BE

At a shout from Zach, I glanced up. He was fifty yards away, jabbing a finger at me.

"Look out! It's headed your way!"

I heard a mewing sound, and turning toward where a finger of forest poked at the shore, I saw a bear cub waddling toward me. A black bear cub, so cute and adorable I grinned in delight. Apparently, it was making for the lake to drink.

"Get out of there!" Zach hollered.

The cub had its head low to the ground and was mewing and grunting as bears often do. It did not realize I was there until I reined my mount to one side. Instantly, it stopped, rose onto its hind legs, and let out with the most awful cry. Almost immediately the undergrowth crackled and snapped, and out of the woods flew four hundred pounds of motherly fury.

Recent books in the Wilderness series:

For a full listing, turn to the back of this book.

WILDERNESS #55:

INTO THE UNKNOWN

David Thompson

LEISURE BOOKS NEW YORK CITY

Dedicated to Judy, Shane, Joshua and Kyndra.

A LEISURE BOOK®

March 2008

Published by

Dorchester Publishing Co., Inc.
200 Madison Avenue
New York, NY 10016

ISBN 10: 0-8439-5931-2
ISBN 13: 978-0-8439-5931-4

Visit us on the web at www.dorchesterpub.com.

WILDERNESS #55:

INTO THE UNKNOWN

AUTHOR'S NOTE

As devoted readers of the popular *Wilderness* series are aware, most of the stories in the saga are based on Nate King's journal. His daughter started a diary in her teen years, and that too has been used. Nate's wife also kept a record, but she wrote the least of the three.

None were day-by-day accounts. The Kings only wrote when the whim moved them. Nate, when something had an impact on his family. Evelyn, when events stirred her emotions or simply to record her thoughts. There is no rhyme or reason to Winona's account.

Other sources have included the journals and diaries of settlers, mountain men and explorers. Wilderness #41: *By Duty Bound,* for instance, was based on the journal of Lieutenant Phillip J. Pickforth.

The author brings all this up because the book you hold in your hands is based on Robert Parker's account of his travels and experiences. A contemporary of John James Audubon, Parker was a naturalist and a painter. His renderings of wildlife, the wilderness, and the Native Americans and white men who inhabited it, are authentic and stunning.

Parker's work is so well known that it needs no introduction. And, too, our story is concerned with only a short interval in his exploration of the West, namely, the month or so he spent with the Kings and the McNairs.

Purists, I trust, will understand why the excerpts early on are abbreviated. The main focus of this story is the King family and their friends.

Chapter One

I am bubbling with excitement! It is the most wonderful news! My patron, the marquis, has decided to fund the expedition. The irony does not elude me. I have never liked painting portraits. I only do it in lean times so I can purchase paint and canvas and food. But he is so enamored of the portrait I did of his wife that he insisted on helping me fulfill my long-cherished ambition to explore the vast uncharted regions west of the Mississippi River.

It is a dream come true! I will venture where few white men have ever dared tread and capture on canvas the wonders my eyes behold. And I have no doubt there will be wonders. The frontier teems with animals and men about which little is known.

Miller and Bodmer have been there before me, and I do not deny that both deserve the accolades heaped on them for their magnificent works. I confess to liking Miller's more, if only because his paintings are imbued with the romance of life, and I have always been a romantic at heart. I cannot possibly put into words how deeply moved I was by his Green River painting. The river, the mist, the mountains, the Indians, it is all so wonderfully sublime.

Still, I must give Bodmer his due. He is a realist. His paintings show exactly what his eyes saw. No sentimentalist, he was ruthless in his depictions of life in the raw. When you look at his Mandans, it is as if you are standing right next to them.

If I can do half as well as Miller and Bodmer, I will justify my talent.

St. Louis, April 2

The preparations continue apace.

There is so much to do, so many details, large and small, to attend to. Men, supplies, horses, all must be acquired. I try to keep expenditures to a minimum in order not to impose too greatly on the marquis's generous nature.

His wife was most indiscreet last night. Collette kept glancing down the table at me. Perhaps the marquis did not notice since he was, as always, deep in his cups. But some of the other guests did. I am sure of it. Now there will be talk, and if the gossip should get back to him, my expedition might be in jeopardy. He would be well within his rights to withdraw his patronage. But as I say, I am a romantic, and I cannot help myself.

In any event, midway through the meal Collette fixed her exquisite hazel eyes on me and said ever so sweetly, "While I am thankful my husband is providing the funds for your exploration of the wilderness, I wonder whether either of you have given any thought to the possible consequences."

"Consequences, my dear?" the marquis asked.

"Specifically the dangers," Collette said. "I very much fear his life will be in constant peril."

What was the woman thinking? Could she be any more transparent? I sought to keep my features inscrutable as I replied, "While I am grateful for your concern, you make much ado over nothing, madam."

"Are wild beasts so trifling then?" she shot back. "Are red savages of no import? Or those tempests of storm and wind I have read about?"

God, how I boiled. Her tone suggested more concern than was proper. I caught a few glances exchanged by others on both sides of the table. The marquis, thankfully, appeared to be oblivious to her impropriety.

"Honestly, my dear. Our friend is eager to be off. It is, as he calls it, an adventure of a lifetime. Would you gainsay him his ambition?"

"Of course not," Collette said tartly. "But neither would I care to lose so dear a friend to the arrows and lances of bloodthirsty heathens or the fangs and claws of a fierce beast."

I regretted then my incurable romanticism. If I would stick to the painting and only the painting, my life would be a lot less complicated. But when a man is in close proximity to a beautiful woman hour after hour and day after day, and when that beautiful woman shows an interest, what is a man to do? I am human, after all.

Fortunately, the marquis took it in a most humorous vein. He laughed long and loud, much longer and much louder than I thought was called for, and then he winked at her and winked at me and said in a jovial fashion, "Far be it for us to stand in the way of our friend's desire. That he is content to risk his life in the furtherance of his art is enough for me. I daresay that if he perishes, it will be for a worthy cause."

It seemed to me he spoke with uncommon relish, and his grin was, for him, peculiar. But I accepted his accolade and assured all and sundry that I was indeed eager to pit myself against the vast unkown.

Fort Leavenworth, May 1

Concern for my welfare is contagious.

This evening I was invited to supper with the officers. Colonel Templeton has proven to be considerate and kindly. He even went so far as to offer to send twenty soldiers as an escort, but I respectfully declined. I deem it prudent to avoid any suggestion that the military is at all connected with my expedition. For one thing, a number of Indian tribes regard the army with a jaundiced eye and are prone to attack units in uniform on general principle. For another, thanks to the marquis's largesse, my party already comprises eight able-bodied men, not including myself. They are well armed with both weapons and fortitude, and, I warrant, will prove more than adequate to deal with any hostilities.

In addition to the colonel, I was introduced to captains Hindeman, Keane and Dugan, and half a dozen lieutenants. The latter let their superiors do most of the talking, and I cannot recall any of their names except for one, a Lieutenant Pickforth, who struck me as an exceedingly opinionated and obtuse individual. To his credit, he has been where I have not, across the nigh limitless prairie to the distant Rockies, and returned alive to tell the tale. At Colonel Templeton's bidding, Pickforth related his various escapades. Perhaps it was the colonel's way of acquainting me with the dangers ahead without having to resort to a lecture. I admire his tact.

Pickforth had many interesting experiences. That herds of buffalo can be a million strong is now common knowledge, but to talk to someone who has seen such a herd and to hear his firsthand account brings the reality that much nearer. And, too, his patrol's clash with a band of hostile Piegans had to be harrowing in the extreme, and was, I suspect, the point Colonel Templeton was trying to make through his proxy.

It irritates me to be considered stupid. Does everyone honestly think I am going into this with my eyes closed? I am fully cognizant that scores, nay, hundreds of people have been slain by Indians, but I am also cognizant that hundreds more have gone into the domain of the red man and come back out again with nary a scratch.

The key is to avoid regions roamed by hostiles and travel only through country where friendly tribes reign. The Shoshones, to name just one example, are widely viewed as perhaps the friendliest tribe of all. Whites in their territory are always welcome and not treated as intruders. The Crows are almost as noteworthy, and, from what I am told, the handsomest of all the red race. One officer was of the opinion they are prone to petty thievery, but others said that was mere myth.

When I inquired if more tribes are friendly than are hostile, I was assured the opposite is the case. The Sioux, or Dakotas as some call them, universally resent white inroads. The implacable hatred of the Blackfoot Confederacy is well established. The Arikaras, the Cheyenne and others have risen against whites from time to time.

From what the officers told me, I am glad I intend to focus my naturalistic forays on the central Rockies. To the north are the aforementioned Blackfeet, to the south the dreaded Comanches and highly feared Apaches.

To be candid, I find the whole conflict insipid. The press paints the red man as the bane of white existence, yet I cannot help but think that they were here before us. And, too, when one white country is encroached on by another white country, bloodshed inevitably results; how is that any different from the situation on the frontier?

Hatred and war hold no interest for me. Nor, I must again be honest, do the politics of what has recently been called our presumed "Manifest Destiny." I do not hate others because their skin is different from mine. I do not believe that my being white, which is, after all, a random chance of birth, entitles me to live where I will and as I will and displace or exterminate anyone who stands in the way of my doing so.

Why can't everyone simply get along? I know, I know. I am being simplistic, and not a little naïve. It is not the nature of the human brute to extend the hand of friendship unless it serves the brute's self-interest. Intellectually that is shallow; morally that is bankrupt.

I would have truck with none of it.

Give me life in all its varied guises. Give me the means to paint it and record it. Give me the opportunity to expand the borders of our knowledge and to open new vistas. Is that too much to ask?

I apologize. I digress. I try to be objective in my journal, but as you can see I do not always succeed.

In any event, the whole conflict is moot as far as I am concerned. A week from now I will be well out on the prairie. I will be doing that which I love best to do. All the rest of it, the bigotry and pretensions and, yes, the silliness, will become as insubstantial as the air.

I can't wait.

Somewhere on the Great American Desert, May 19

I do not know where I am. It is glorious.

I should know. But the crate containing our sextant

is at the bottom of the Mississippi River, and I refused to spend a week or more camped on the west bank while one of my men went back to try and procure another. Ignorance as to our exact longitude and latitude hinders us only slightly. So long as we can ascertain the four points of the compass—and of those we brought several—we can get by with more than tolerable efficiency.

I should be thankful. The mishap that sent the crate containing some of our equipment into the river might well have sent my paints and brushes and easel. *That* would be a calamity of the first order. I can get by without knowing where in heaven's name I am, but it would be pointless to continue without the means to capture on canvas that which I come across.

And there is so much to see! To say the animal life is abundant is to say the ocean is deep or the sky is high. Our scout and chief hunter, Augustus Trevor, says this will change, that game becomes so scarce we will be fortunate if we do not starve. He has crossed the prairie several times so I trust his judgment. When he advised me to lay up a store of dried meat, that is exactly what we did.

I must make a decision. My supply of paint and canvas is limited. Do I paint every animal and new plant we encounter here on the plains, or do I contain my enthusiasm so that I have plenty of canvas and paper left when I reach the mountains? The answer is obvious.

Still, I can't not paint.

A pair of white-tailed rabbits are too adorable to ignore. They are as fluffy and soft as pillows, with appealing yellow eyes and long ears tipped with black triangles. How can I not paint them, when they are not found east of the Mississippi?

The same with a coyote Trevor shot. Yes, we have coyotes galore in the States, but this one was three times the size of any coyote I ever beheld or heard of, almost a wolf in stature and worth the expenditure of precious paint.

Then there are the birds. My God, the birds!

Of all the creatures in creation, I confess I am partial to our avian friends. I don't know whether it is that I have always envied their power of flight, or that their delightfully diverse plumage presents such a formidable challenge and such lasting satisfaction if my brush does them justice.

You might think, given how generally flat the prairie is and the relative absence of trees, that birds would have nowhere to roost and thus be rare, but I can confirm that their abundance is second only to their variety.

You who are reading this journal are probably familiar with the common bluebird, but how about a bird with a vivid blue head and blue wings, gray throat and orange body? Or a bird with a yellow crown and yellow throat and yellow rings around the wings and the tail, and a melodious warble that is a joy to the ears? Or an oriole that is similar to the Baltimore variety but has splashes of orange on both sides of its head and above its eyes?

Vicinity of the Platte River, June 2

We have had an incident.

The previous night we camped on the bank of the Platte, as we have been doing for some days now while we follow it generally westward. I cannot help but think that calling the Platte a river is a slur on rivers everywhere. That a waterway so shallow and sluggish and narrow should be designated as such amazes and amuses me. But it is water, and after nearly perishing from thirst before we reached it, I should be grateful and not carp.

But to the incident.

We had a fire going and our sixteen horses tethered in a string under guard. Our sleep was undisturbed until about an hour before dawn. Then the sentry, who happened to be young Billingsley, and who by his own admission was so tired he could scarcely keep his eyes open, heard a sound that brought his head up. Not a loud sound, by any means, but the suggestion of a stealthy tread. Since deer and other animals sometimes pass close by in the night, Billingsley did not think much of it and lowered his chin to his chest.

Then one of the horses nickered, and a second stamped, and Billingsley looked up again to find the entire string alert, with their heads high and their ears pricked. Clearly something was amiss for the entire string to be agitated. He moved toward them, cradling his rifle. He says that he thought they had caught the scent of a prowling bear or catamount, and he spoke softly to them to quiet them so they would not wake the rest of us.

One of the horses pulled at the picket rope. Billingsley started down the string, then stopped. He had spied what he described as strange shadow on the ground near the horse that stamped. He could not see it clearly enough to tell what it was. From its size, he judged it to be an animal, a coyote perhaps, or a fox, although why either would venture so near puzzled him.

Billingsley brought the stock of his rifle to his shoulder and took another step, and it was then that the mundane turned into the remarkable, for the shadow suddenly unfolded and swelled in size, taking on the dimensions of a man.

Billingsley was so startled, he was a few seconds collecting his wits. He was slow to recognize the half-naked form for what it was. But the long hair, the breechclout, the suggestion of paint on the angular face, could leave no doubt. The figure moved, and the glint of metal in its hand told Billingsley the whole story and shocked him out of his lethargy. With a holler of, "Indians! Indians!" he took a bead, but as quick as he was, our nocturnal visitor was faster. With a bound, the red man vanished into the greenery.

By then the rest of us were roused. I came out from under my blankets swiftly enough, but had to fumble about to find my pistol. I had not kept it close to me despite our scout's repeated advice. Some of the others were likewise lax. It was the hand of Providence that we were not under attack, for we could not have rallied to defend ourselves in time to prevent our being massacred. But find the pistol I did, and I immediately rushed to Billingsley's aid. He had run to the edge of the clearing but did not plunge into the woods after our visitor.

Augustus Trevor congratulated the young man on his caution. Trevor said that where there was one there were bound to be more, and if Billingsley had given chase, he might have run into the waiting arms of a war party and suffered torture and mutilation.

To his credit, young Billingsley made no pretensions to wisdom. He said it was fear, not caution, that brought him to a stop.

On examination, we found that the warrior had been in the act of cutting the horses free, with the intent of stealing them, when he was interrupted by Billingsley. The rope was, in fact, half severed. A few more seconds, and we might well have been stranded on foot—a calamity, Trevor states, of the highest order.

None of us were able to go back to sleep. More wood was thrown on the fire until the blaze cast light twice as far as before. A new batch of coffee was brewed, and until sunrise we sat drinking and watching, every man armed with all his weapons.

Life's ironies are limitless. I had begun to question the widespread dread in which the red man is held. To hear some people talk, a hate-filled savage lurks behind every bush and tree. But for weeks now we had been crossing the land of the red man and not seen a trace of that race. Proof, to my mind, that the common fear of Indians is as exaggerated as it is misguided. Now this.

Perhaps I am the one who has been misguided. Perhaps the dangers are more real than I believed.

If so, what does that bode for the future?

Chapter Two

The Prairie, June 12

All right.

I admit it.

There is no "perhaps" about the dangers. There is no "perhaps" about the prospect of dying.

We have left the Platte behind. We followed it to where it forked. The north fork would have taken us toward South Pass and the Green River country, made famous by the exploits of those hardy souls who engaged in the fur trade until beaver went out of fashion. We took the south fork, for a few days, anyway, and then our scout said that we must strike straight off across the prairie to a trading post known as Bent's Fort.

I cannot get over the vastness of this grassland. I have never been on board a ship in the middle of the ocean, but I have heard that it gives one a sense of the limitlessness of the briny deep. The same can be applied to the prairie. It seems to go on forever, a sea of grass without end. We who traverse it are but tiny specks adrift in its immensity.

Yesterday afternoon we passed close to mounds of earth pockmarked with burrows. A prairie dog town,

Trevor said, and he advised us to give it a wide berth as many a horse has broken a leg by inadvertently stepping into one of the holes. We complied, but I had barely reined after him when there came a sound as of seeds being shaken in a dry gourd, and the next I knew, my mount whinnied and reared and it was all I could do to stay in the saddle.

Belatedly, I recognized the sound for what it was: the telltale warning of a rattlesnake. I glanced down and perceived sinuous movement, but then had my hands full regaining control of my steed. Trevor and the others rushed to my assistance. I am proud to say I did not need it, and with a few pats and soft-spoken words, my animal's calm was restored.

As for the serpent, it slithered off into a prairie dog hole before anyone could shoot it. Trevor informed us that rattlesnakes are often found near prairie dog colonies, prairie dog litters being high on the snake's list of delicacies.

Today dawned sunny and warm. By nine I was sweating; by noon I was sweltering. Nary a tree nor any other cover within sight and the temperature by our thermometer was one hundred and one.

About the middle of the afternoon a bank of dark clouds appeared to the north. Soon we saw the flash of lightning and a nebulous mist between the dark clouds and the ground that signified a deluge. A thunderhead, but as it was drifting from west to east and we were well to the south of it, we gave it no more thought than we had countless others.

Trevor turned to me and said, "You will be happy to hear that in three or four days we should reach Bent's Fort."

Welcome news, indeed. The trading post is the last bastion of civilization before the mountains. We intend to spend a week resting and recuperating, then purchase new provisions and strike off into unexplored territory.

Presently, a distant rumble fell on my ears. I equated it with thunder from the storm and rode blithely on until our scout suddenly drew rein and shifted in the saddle.

"What is the matter?" I asked, struck by what might be alarm on his face.

"I hope I am wrong," he said. Rising in the stirrups, he peered intently to the north.

It occurs to me as I write this that I have not described him. Imagine rawhide made flesh. He has lived on the frontier most of his adult life, and the imprint of hardship and the elements are stamped on his rugged features. The one word I would choose for his character is *tough*. His age I would not presume to guess, for while he exhibits the vitality of a twenty-year-old, he has enough gray hairs to persuade me he is at least twice that age.

Anyway, we rode on, but we had only gone a short way when Trevor again drew rein. This time there was no doubt about his alarm, for the others saw it, too.

"What is it?" asked Wilson, our cook.

"Don't you have ears?" Trevor responded. "Can't you hear?"

"Hear what?"

"That rumbling."

"The storm, you mean?" young Billingsley said.

"Would that it were," Trevor said, and glanced all about us, as if he were seeking something.

"What else can it be?" Billingsley inquired.

"Our doom," Trevor said.

Since I was the leader of the expedition I felt compelled to say, "Confound it man, speak plainly. What has you so agitated?"

"We must find cover, and we must find it quickly," Trevor replied, and jabbed his heels against his mount.

We had no choice but to hurry after him. I was anxious to question him further, but he had brought his animal to a gallop and I would have to shout to be heard. He was heading to the southwest at a breakneck clip. Repeatedly, he looked over his shoulder, and each time he did, he scowled.

I was at a loss. The rumbling still sounded to my ears like thunder. Then I noticed that it was becoming louder, which was odd, since we were putting more distance between the thunderstorm and ourselves. Logic dictated the sound should grow fainter. Obviously, then, the rumble was *not* thunder. And whatever it was, was coming closer by the moment.

I glanced to the north.

For a few moments the sight I beheld made no sense. There appeared to be a second dark cloud bank, only this one was close to the ground and flowing toward us at a startling speed.

Soon I saw that what I had taken for a single mass was instead made up of many small parts. Not in the scores or the hundreds or even the thousands, but in numbers too great too count. I saw, too, that each of these parts possessed a pair of curved horns and a hump and four flying hooves.

They were buffalo.

A herd, God knew how large, had been stampeded by lightning or some other cause and were bearing down on us like a shaggy avalanche.

My analogy leaves a little to be desired, but the end result, should they overtake us, would be the same; we would be crushed under tons of bone, sinew and horn, pulverized to pieces and left for the buzzards to feast on. No one would ever know our fate, not unless at some future date a wayfarer happened on a few of our bleached bones.

Morbid thoughts, I confess, but under the circumstances they were justified.

We lashed our mounts, to no avail. The buffalo continued to gain. I have since learned that when in flight, they are as tireless as Titans. A fitting description, given that the males weigh upward of a ton and stand six feet high at the shoulder.

I cannot say how far we fled. Mile after mile, to the point where my dun was flecked with sweat and flagging, and many of the other horses were about done in.

It was then that Trevor rose in the stirrups and pointed, shouting, "Over yonder! As you value your hides, stay with me!"

I needed no urging. The buffalo were less than two hundred yards behind us, a roiling maelstrom that obliterated everything in its path. The rumbling had become a thunderous din, and from under their pounding hooves swirled a thick column of dust.

What strange creatures men are. I say that because my life was in the direst peril, but I was not thinking of that. I was thinking only of my art supplies and equipment. I saw Jeffers frantically tugging on the lead rope to the pack animals. Burdened as they were, they were falling behind.

What I did next surprised even me.

I wheeled the dun. Trevor shouted my name, but I did not answer. I raced back to Jeffers and hauled on the reins to bring the dun in close to the pack animals. With yells and motions I sought to hasten their flight, and in that I succeeded, for they moved faster.

I looked up in time to witness an incredible sight; our scout seemed to ride into the ground itself. One by one the other men did the same, vanishing before my eyes.

Thirty more yards, the miracle was explained.

Long ago a cataclysm had rent the earth leaving a gash some ten feet wide and about that deep. At the bottom were my men, hastily dismounting.

Trevor bellowed to bring their rifles and follow him.

I was the last to descend. They were climbing back up and I passed them on the way down. Before the dun came to a stop, I was off and after them.

Trevor reached the rim and sank to one knee. He immediately pressed the stock of his rifle to his shoulder.

I did not need to ask what he was about to shoot, although why he would bother mystified me. There were eight of us and hundreds of thousands of buffalo. Dropping a few would have no more effect than dipping a finger into raging rapids to stem the flow of a river.

But Trevor was determined to try. "Aim for the ones coming right at us!" he roared. "Wait until I give the word, then squeeze trigger!"

"What good will this do us?" Wilson wanted to know.

Trevor did not answer. His cheek was to his rifle. We imitated him.

I am not much of a shot. In childhood I hunted, but my heart was never in it. Even today, I would rather paint specimens alive than dead, but that simply is not practical so I have others do my shooting for me.

But now my aversion was moot. A living wall of horn and muscle was bearing down on us. I swear the very ground shook. My mouth was dry, and my palms grew slick. I firmed my grip and waited for Trevor to give the command to fire.

"Remember, aim for the buffs coming right at us!"

A futile exercise, I reflected, since behind the first rank were untold more. But I centered my Hawken's sights between a bull's beady eyes and thumbed back the hammer.

At times, heartbeats can become hours. This was one of them. The buffalo seemed to be moving in slow motion. I saw the flair of every nostril, the driving thrust of every hoof. The illusion lasted all of ten seconds, and then they were on top of us and everything happened so swiftly and so furiously that the details are a bit of a haze even if the sequence is not.

"Fire!" Trevor cried, and fire we did, our eight rifles blasting almost in unison. Only Trevor and Jeffers could claim to be marksmen of any note, but the buffalo were so close that marksmanship was not much of a factor.

Our eight rifles boomed. Six buffalo crashed down. They struck hard, and rolled or tumbled or slid to a rest near the edge. In doing so they formed a barrier between us and the onrushing herd, which I divined was Trevor's intent. Almost instantly the herd parted, breaking to the right and the left, going around the bodies of their fallen fellows.

A temporary reprieve at best, I thought. The press of massive forms would soon drive the living against the dead and both the dead and the living would spill into our sanctuary. They would crush all us tiny humans who had the temerity to try and stem the tide of certain death.

Trevor was scrambling toward the horses. "Get back!" he bellowed. "Get away from the rim!"

I barely heard him, the din was so loud. How can I

describe the indescribable? Imagine you are surrounded by a million men pounding the ground with
heavy hammers, and you will have some idea. Add to
that the riot of snorts, grunts and cries from a legion
of bison throats. The walls of our retreat trembled,
and the air was chocked with dust.

I pictured our broken bodies lying under a heap of
thrashing buffalo. I cursed my arrogance in believing
that somehow I was special, for thinking that the
wilderness would single me out for the unique honor
of immunity from its many dangers.

It is ever so. We think bad things will happen to
others but not to us. The life breathed into us is somehow different from the breath of life in everyone else.
Ours cannot be extinguished by random happen-
stance. We are special.

A common delusion, I daresay.

I am not overly religious, and I make no claim to
understanding Scripture better than anyone else, but
there is a quote that has stuck with me and sums up
the state of our existence to a remarkable degree. *He
sends rain on the just and the unjust*, or something to
that effect. Could it possibly be any clearer? None of
us merit special treatment. We are one and the same
with everyone else. We are fodder in the panorama of
life. Nothing more, nothing less.

My morbid streak is showing again.

But back to that cleft in the earth, and to the buffalo
and the dust and the fear that coursed through my
veins. I made it to the bottom and helped the others
hold fast to our horses, which were in a state of sheer
terror and fit to bolt. They plunged and reared and
whinnied.

Along both rims flowed endless shaggy forms with
their bulging humps and wicked black horns. On and

on, until my nerves were raw and my mind numb and I could barely breathe for the dust in the air.

We never forget certain moments in our lives. Moments so profound, so intense, they are indelibly seared into our being. Such it was with me when Augustus Trevor hollered, "The worst is over!"

He was right. The thunder was not as loud. The snorting and grunting was less. The herd was thinning.

I clung to the reins on my mount and to the rope to the pack animals, and I could have wept for joy. The only reason I didn't, I suppose, is that I was too dazed. The blank expressions of the others showed they were in the same state.

At length the ground stopped trembling, the dust stopped swirling, and the thunder ceased altogether.

Trevor was first to stir and climb to the top. He raised his head above the rim and gazed about him with the air of someone who does not believe what he is seeing. Then he beckoned.

I do not know what I expected. Pockmarked earth, yes, and to find that in places the grass had been pounded down to bare dirt. I had not counted on the bodies, though. Mostly cows and calves but I also spied a few old bulls. They had tripped or stumbled or tired and gone down, never to rise again. Brown mounds ringed by red, some so badly mangled I honestly could not tell that they had been buffalo.

"It's a miracle!" Wilson exclaimed. "The Lord be praised!" He shook his pudgy hands at the sky, his belly jiggling.

"We live!" young Billingsley marveled. "We still live!" He jumped up and down in glee.

I shared their relief, but more so that my supplies had been spared than that we had. That might seem hard-hearted, but I am a naturalist, after all, and my easel and my sketchbooks are my means of recording my endeavors for posterity.

Soon we were underway.

Once again the dangers I had taken so lightly had shown they were not to be mocked. Either I learned my lesson, or I perished.

It was that simple.

Chapter Three

We have arrived at an oasis of civilization in the middle of nowhere.

Since Trevor repeatedly referred to it as a fort, I had envisioned a structure along military lines, even though he stressed it was civilian run, and had never been anything but a trading center.

I can think of no better way to convey what I beheld than to say it was a castle made of mud. Adobe, the style is called, a word of Spanish extraction. More aesthetic than logs, it lent an atmosphere of dignity and sophistication to what was essentially a site where beads, trinkets and liquor were traded for furs.

How they ever built it with a relative handful of men, I cannot conceive. I would have thought an army would be required.

The dimensions were as follows: the front and rear walls were approximately one hundred and forty feet in length, the side nearer one hundred and eighty. The average height was fourteen feet, and all the walls were three feet thick. They were proof not only against rifles and pistols and arrows, but a cannon ball would not penetrate.

As if that were not enough, at the northwest and southeast corners were towers housing cannons.

At its maximum, provided provisions were adequate, the fort could sustain two hundred men and twice that in stock and poultry.

I had to paint it.

I also had to paint the men who ran it.

This remarkable enterprise was the brainchild of the Bent brothers and Ceran St. Vrain. I saw more of the latter than the former, who were busy with freighters bound for Santa Fe.

St. Vrain is an aristocratic gentleman, well-read and kindly yet firm in his dealings with subordinates. It was from his lips that I first heard the names which would soon figure so prominently in my life. It happened when he mentioned having a Cheyenne wife.

"How remarkable," I responded.

"Not really," said he. "Quite a few white men have found Indian maidens much to their liking. Nate King and Joseph Walker are the most famous examples."

I had never heard of either and stated as much.

"Good Lord, man," St. Vrain said. "Walker's explorations are legendary. As for King, he is one of my closest friends and as ideal an example of the mountain man as you are likely to meet."

"The mountain man?"

"That is what people are calling whites who stayed on in the mountains after the beaver trade faded. King was one of the best of the trappers and one of the first whites to go Indian, as they say. His wife is a Shoshone, and I don't mind admitting she is as beauteous a woman as ever drew breath."

"It is a good thing your own wife is not here beside us," I joked. "She might take exception."

"No, she would not," St. Vrain responded good-naturedly. "Winona and my wife are good friends."

An idea occurred to me. "This Nate King knows these mountains well, then, I gather?"

"No one knows them better. He used to live not all that far from here, at the eastern edge of the mountains. But he has since moved deeper in, and we do not see him nearly as often."

"That's too bad," I said. "I would like to meet him."

"I cannot speak highly enough of his character or that of his best friend, Shakespeare McNair."

The name stirred the vaguest of recollections. "I would swear I heard of him when I was a boy."

"You probably did," St. Vrain grinned. "McNair is older than Methuselah. He was one of the first, if not *the* very first white man to ever reach the Rockies. He was here long before beaver drew men in droves."

"Have they any children, King and McNair?"

"Nate King does," St. Vrain said, and his face clouded.

"What?" I prompted.

"Nothing."

"Is there something about them I should know? What if I run into them in my travels?"

"It is only that Nate's son—" St. Vrain began, and caught himself. He gazed about us at the bustle of activity, then lowered his voice. "Zach King is his name. A nice enough lad, so long as you stay on his good side. The taint of being a breed has scarred him and made him more vicious than he would be otherwise, in my estimation."

"Because he has a white father and a red mother?"

"Exactly that, yes. Halfbreeds are held in low esteem on the frontier, or anywhere else, for that matter. Most whites regard them as prone to violence, and many Indians do not want anything to do with them because they are considered bad medicine."

"Are the opinions justified?"

"Oh, please. We are men of culture, you and I. We know superstition when we hear it. My own children are half-and-half, and they are as kind and as ordinary as any of so-called purer blood." St. Vrain shook his head. "No, the stigma attached to breeds is uncalled for."

"But you say this Zach King has a vicious disposition?"

"A poor choice of words on my part," St. Vrain said. "Yes, Zach has a reputation. But his violence has always been provoked. Under normal circumstances he is as peaceable as you or I."

I was not entirely convinced. His expression hinted at darker underpinnings. But I deemed it of no consequence since I never intended to make Zach King's acquaintance. I was intrigued by the father, though. Nate King's intimate knowledge of the mountains might surpass that of Augustus Trevor.

Bent's Fort, June 19

This was the day I would paint the trading post. What with an encampment of Crows nearby and a wagon train that had arrived the day before drawn up in a circle outside the walls, the painting promised to be picturesque.

Bright and early I gathered what I needed and made for the gate. Young Billingsley was waiting outside the quarters St. Vrain had graciously provided, and I burdened him with my easel.

Augustus Trevor had wanted to go along, with two or three others for extra protection, but I scoffed at the suggestion. I was only hiking a short way, I insisted, and I would be within hailing distance of the armed sentries stationed on the ramparts. Trevor relented, but only after I agreed to take one of the men. I chose Billingsley. He always did my bidding without question. Consequently, no sooner did we hike a suitable distance than I told him I did not need his services and he was free to spend the rest of the day as he saw fit. He protested, saying Trevor had been quite specific about not leaving me, but I pointed out that I was the leader of our expedition, not Mr. Trevor, and my word was final.

I think that secretly Billingsley was glad to have time to himself. He capitulated and scooted toward the post with a grin.

I was happy, too. At last, at long, long last, I was alone.

An explanation is called for.

I am not the most sociable of men. Human company tends to pale after a while. I value solitude as some men value gold, and I had enjoyed precious little of it since the expedition's start. During our crossing of the prairie I was never alone. I rode at their side during the day, while at night their constant snores reminded me of their presence. Whenever I was inclined to venture off alone to paint or explore, Trevor always had at least one man go with me.

"You hired me to not only serve as your guide, Mr. Parker, but to bring you back to civilization safe and hale, and that is exactly what I intend to do, with or without your cooperation."

While I admired Trevor's devotion to duty, I was frustrated to no end by the lack of privacy.

At Bent's Fort the situation was compounded many

times over. Yes, St. Vrain graciously gave me a room, but I neglected to mention it was in use as a supply room, and he had his employees clean it out so I would have a niche of my own. A niche it was, too, with barely enough room for the cot he had his people fetch. There were no windows, only four close walls. During the day it was stifling and at night little better. I used it only for sleep, and then only to be polite to my host.

So here I was, outside the Fort and on my own. I promptly gathered my supplies and my easel and hiked to the northwest. I wanted to capture the entire post, including the picturesque teepees and the circle of wagons. For the proper perspective I needed to be as far from everything as practical.

I hummed to myself as I strolled along. The day was hot but not unbearably so. A sluggish breeze brought licks of relief now and again.

I was not worried about the Crows. Their camp was hundreds of yards to the south, and they paid no more attention to white men wandering about than they would to birds or butterflies. Besides which, they would never cause trouble so near the fort. The brothers and St. Vrain had an inviolate rule: trouble-makers were banished from trading, the length of the banishment depending on the severity of their misconduct. Not only that, the troublemaker's tribe was also banned. To the Indians, many of whom depended on the post for trade articles they could not obtain anywhere else, being banned was a calamity of the first order. As a result, the tribes were always on their best behavior.

Bent's Fort was a neutral zone where animosities were forgotten in the interest of the greater good for all. Thus it was that on occasion tribes at war with one another showed up at the trading post at the same time yet coexisted in perfect harmony for the duration of their stay. Once they were back in their own territories, they resumed killing one another with savage abandon.

I ask you, is there anything more fickle than human nature? And no, I am not singling out the red man in this regard. The white man is equally guilty of slaughtering his brothers and sisters on the flimsiest of pretexts. We, too, have our truces and our periods of peace, but has there ever been a time in our history when somewhere on the globe a war was not being waged and blood was not being spilled by the gallon?

If I sound cynical, it is only because I am. I have lost much of my faith in my fellow man. I prefer the honest beasts of the forest and the field to the devious beasts of city and town who preach love but practice lies, deceit, and carnage on a scale to stagger the mind.

Again I have digressed.

I came to a likely spot on a low mound about a quarter of a mile from the fort, and there set up my easel. I was still humming, which might account for why I did not hear the riders until they were a stone's throw away. I glanced around sharply, saw they were white men, and went back to work. I was not so cynical that I distrusted every living soul on sight.

I expected the riders to go on their way to the trading post, and I gave them no more thought until I had an odd feeling I was being watched. I was mildly surprised to find the trio had reined up and were regarding me as I might regard an albino antelope. "Gentlemen," I said cordially, and went back to my canvas.

"What in tarnation are you fixing to do, mister?"

Without looking to see which one had spoken, I

replied, "I should think it is obvious. I am about to paint."

"No fooling?"

"I am very much in earnest, yes."

"Where did you come from?" another inquired.

"East of the Mississippi, where most everyone comes from," I responded. "Now if you will excuse me, I want to get this done before the sun goes down." I thought that would be the end of it and applied the brush with delicate strokes. I was so absorbed, I did not realize they had dismounted until a shadow fell across me. I glanced up.

They were scruffy specimens, these newcomers. Granted, most frontiersmen are always in need of a bath and their clothes in need of washing, but these three apparently considered cleanliness a state to be avoided at all costs. Their hair was greasy, their beards unkempt. Their buckskins were fit to be burned. All three bristled with weapons. Their hard, almost cruel faces betrayed not so much as a hint of friendliness.

"Gentlemen," I said again. "What can I do for you? Perhaps you did not hear me, but I am busy."

"Oh, we heard you, all right," said the man in the center. He was of middling height and build, not the least bit remarkable in any respect except for his dark eyes, which glittered in a disturbing fashion. "And I can't say I cared for your tone."

"I meant no disrespect," I said, and introduced myself.

"I'm Jess Hook," the man revealed. "This ugly cuss on my right is my brother, Jordy. Our ma was partial to names that begin with J."

His sibling was distinguished by a nose as huge as I ever beheld. It reminded me of a bird of prey's beak. I smiled but received only a cold stare.

"This other coon is Cutter."

The man in question had a knife on each hip and another wedged under his belt near the buckle. Thin and wiry, he sported a vivid scar that ran from his right ear to his chin. At one time he had apparently been dealt a fearsome blow. In healing, the skin pinched inward, so that half his face was disfigured. His eyes were flat and lifeless. The only thing I can think to compare them to were the eyes of a shark I once saw that had been netted and hung on a dock.

"Is that his first or his last name?" I asked.

"Neither. It is just what we call him," Jess Hook said. He gazed toward Bent Fort's, then at me. "Didn't anyone tell you it's not safe to be by your lonesome in these parts?"

Only then did it hit me how far I had walked. The trading post was uncomfortably distant. "I warrant the sentries can still see me," I remarked. "And you," I added for emphasis.

"Maybe so," Jess said. "But this far out, they can't tell who we are."

The man called Cutter casually placed a hand near the knife close to his buckle.

Chapter Four

"See here," I said. "What exactly do you want with me?"

"I haven't rightly decided yet," Jess Hook said, and stepping up, he dared to press a finger to the canvas and then stared at the paint on the tip of his finger.

Now, if there is one thing I cannot abide, it is to have my canvases touched. I do not get as hot about it when the paint has dried, but when the paint is fresh, the slightest contact causes a smudge or smear I must work diligently to correct. Accordingly, without any consideration for the consequences, I smacked his arm away, saying, "Don't do that!"

Jess Hook looked at me in amazement. "Did you see that, boys?" he said to his companions. "Did you see what this fancy pants just did?"

"I sure did, brother," Jordy Hook said. "Some folks don't have no more brains than a tree stump."

Cutter's hand slid to the knife and wrapped around the hilt. "Want me to gut him for you, Jess?"

I took a step back, my brush in one hand, the palette in the other. "Enough of this childish talk," I gruffly declared. "I am engaged in serious work, and I will not be interrupted."

"Is that a fact?" Jess Hook smirked. "Mister, I don't know about where you come from, but in these parts, when you hit someone, it can be worth your teeth, or more."

"I will not be threatened," I said.

"Then you shouldn't treat folks the way you do," Jess Hook said. He lowered a hand to a pistol, and his manner became icy. "I have decided I don't like you much."

"Let's be reasonable," I said, seeking to make amends. "We are grown men, after all. You go your way and leave me to my work."

"You don't listen too good," Jess Hook said. "We are of no account to you, is that it?"

"I do not take your meaning."

Jess Hook poked me in the chest. "You are one of those who reckons he's better'n everyone else. I've met your kind before, and there's only one way to treat snobs like you."

"Now see here," I began, but got no further. They had spread out to surround me. It was ominous in the extreme.

"What do you say, boys?" Jess Hook said. "Should we whittle on him to teach him some respect?"

"I want one of his ears to add to my collection," Jordy said.

"You collect *ears*?" I blurted in horror.

"And other body parts." Jordy grinned and patted the possibles bag slanted across his chest. "My favorite is the part I took off a Blackfoot once. Want to see?"

"Hush, you infant!" Jess snapped. "He looks down his nose at us and you want to show him your collection?"

"I did no such thing," I said, but they ignored me. I entertained the idea that this was a joke on their part, a poor joke, it is true, but in keeping with the coarse humor for which frontiersmen are generally known. Then Cutter drew his knife and held it so the blade gleamed in the sun.

"Enough jawing. Let's cart him off where we can have our fun in private. I want to cut nice and slow so—" He gazed past me and blinked.

"What is it?" Jeff Hook said, turning.

Someone else had ridden up. A young man, bronzed by the sun to where he could pass for an Indian. On closer scrutiny, I saw he *was* an Indian, in part anyway; his green eyes betrayed the truth. Raven black hair hung loose to his broad shoulders, framing handsome features. His horse was a fine bay. I assumed he was an acquaintance of theirs until Jess Hook addressed him.

"Didn't that pa of yours teach you better than to sneak up on folks, breed?"

The young man had a Hawken rifle in the crook of his left elbow. Almost casually, he pointed it at the Hook brothers and said, "I can't help it if your ears don't work."

"This is a private matter," Jess Hook said.

"Be on your way if you know what is good for you," Jordy Hook angrily added.

The young man was not intimidated. Looking at me, he said, "The problem with fleas is that they come in all shapes and sizes. I can shoo these off if you want me to."

I was slow to catch on that he was offering to help me, then I hastily replied, "Yes. Please. I would be in your debt."

Cutter sidled to one side. He had his rifle in both hands, and was inching it up.

"Stupid is as stupid does," the young man told him.

A strange grin curled Cutter's lips, and he let his arms drop. "You have a point. When it happens, I want to pick the time and place."

"Don't hold off on my account."

Jess Hook's jaw muscles twitched. "Damn you. We won't forget you butting in like this."

"I think we can take him!" Jordy declared. "Say the word, brother, and I'll blow this breed to hell and back."

"What you will do," Jess said, "is forget about him and head for Bent's Fort."

"But we can take him!" Jordy insisted.

At that, Jess took a step and gave his brother a violent push, shoving Jordy so hard he stumbled and nearly fell. "When I tell you to do something, little brother, you damn well better do it."

I thought Jordy would take a swing at him. But the younger sibling merely clenched his fists and stalked in a sulk to his horse. He swung up and without a backward glance, gigged his animal toward the trading post.

Cutter was next to wheel and leave. "Don't get a crick in your neck from looking over your shoulder," he taunted.

Jess Hook smiled. "You made a mistake today, boy."

"I have made them before," the young man said.

"Until we meet again." Jess Hook nodded and walked off.

The young man raised his reins to depart, but I barred his way, saying, "I want to thank you for your assistance. There is no telling what they would have done if you had not shown up."

"Not all rabid wolves have four legs," the young man said, and again went to leave.

"Hold on. Must you go?" I asked. "I would like to

make your acquaintance." I was intensely curious as to who he was, and why he had served as my protector.

"Then you are a rarity, mister," he replied. "Most whites shun halfbreeds as they would lepers."

"I am not a bigot." I indicated my easel. "I have some small skill as an artist, and to an artist all hues are of equal worth."

"Would that all men were artists," the young man said rather wistfully. He jabbed his heels and rode around me toward Bent's. "Maybe we will meet again."

"I hope so!" I called after him, but he gave no heed. I was left alone with my paints and my thoughts. No sooner did I resume painting, however, when another pair of riders came galloping in my direction from Bent's Fort. So much for my being alone. They passed the three hardcases and then my rescuer, and were wearing scowls when they came to a stop.

"What in God's name do you think you were doing?" Augustus Trevor lit into me without dismounting. "It is a good thing I ran into Billingsley. You should not be out here alone."

I did not respond.

"How can we protect you when you refuse to take our advice?" Trevor gestured. "Any one of those four men I just saw would slit your throat and not give it a second thought."

"The young one was nice enough." I did not go into detail about my exchange with the Hooks.

"You are a babe in the woods," Trevor said. "Or in this instance, a babe in the grass." He pointed at the retreating figure of my benefactor. "For your information, that there is one of the worst killers on the frontier."

I refused to believe it. "Hogwash."

"I have seen him a few times, here and there," Trevor elaborated, "so I know what I'm talking about."

"Does this terror have a name?"

"Zach King."

My interest was piqued. So *that* was the fearsome scourge I had heard so much about? His reputation was at odds with his demeanor. "He is not the monster people make him out to be."

Trevor did not hide his frustration with me. "A rattlesnake is peaceable enough until you step on it. Zach King has fangs, and he's not shy about using them. Give thanks he didn't decide to take a bite out of you."

"A curious analogy," I glibly remarked.

"Consarn it, Parker. I can't keep you alive when you think you know better than me. You said that you hired me for my experience, but you refuse to heed."

I had a retort on the tip of my tongue, but I remembered that he only had my best interests at heart. And my brief encounter with the Hook brothers and their knife-loving friend had impressed on me, yet again, that I was not taking this life-or-death business seriously enough.

Trevor and Billingsley remained with me the rest of the afternoon. The sun was low to the horizon when I folded my easel and made ready to head back. The painting turned out well. I did not add as much detail as I would for an animal or plant, say, but I never do with landscapes.

Ceran St. Vrain had invited me to his quarters for supper. I was tired and not all that hungry, and I nearly sent word I could not make it. Fortunately, I rallied and knocked on his door at the appointed hour.

"I hope you won't mind," St. Vrain said as he shook my hand in welcome, "but I invited someone else. The son of one of my dearest friends." He stepped aside.

Who should be seated at the table but Zach King!

"So we meet again," I said, smiling and offering my hand. "Perhaps it is an omen."

Zach rose to greet me, but without any great enthusiasm. "My mother's people believe in signs and portents, but it is not a belief I share."

For a so-called savage he was remarkably eloquent. I sat down to table with the hope of getting to know him better.

St. Vrain's cook had outdone himself. We had our choice of antelope or buffalo, or both. Corn, string beans, potatoes, and bread smeared thick with butter were side dishes. My session on the prairie had made me ravenous, and little was said until we put down our forks and spoons and filled our coffee cups. I smacked my lips in satisfaction, then cleared my throat.

"I have a proposition for you, Mr. King, and I hope you will hear me out." When he did not say anything, I leaped right in. "Ceran tells me that your family lives in a hidden valley deep in the mountains. It is so far back, no other white men have ever been there."

"Except for Shakespeare McNair. We like our privacy."

"Are there a lot of animals?" I asked, recalling full well that their valley had been described to me as an Eden on earth.

"All kinds," Zach confirmed. "More than you will find in any one area in the mountains. My pa says our valley is a throwback to the times when there were no people."

"I would very much like to meet him and McNair. Do you think your father would mind if you took me back with you?"

My request appeared to startle him. "You did hear me say we like our privacy?"

"Surely you make exceptions," I said.

"A few Shoshones and Utes and a Crow have stopped by from time to time." Zach shrugged. "And a few others," he enigmatically added.

"Then there is precedent."

Zach grinned a not unfriendly grin. "You are partial to big words, just like Uncle Shakespeare. Yes, we have had visitors. But they have all been red, not white."

"Then I could be the first white man to visit your valley, could I not?"

Zach glanced sharply at Ceran St. Vrain. I flattered myself I could read his thoughts, and said, "Please don't be annoyed at our host. He did not know I would ask this of you."

"I do not like being imposed on," Zach said bluntly. "What purpose would your visit serve?"

"I would like to paint your valley and everything in it."

"What on earth for?"

"I am a naturalist. I came to the Rockies for the express purpose of cataloging its fauna and flora."

"You can paint anywhere in the mountains," Zach noted. "It does not have to be our valley."

"But you yourself said there are more animals in your valley than anywhere else. Imagine the time and effort that would save me. I need not traipse all over. Everything I could possibly want to paint would be right there."

Zach stalled by sipping coffee. He was not pleased and was trying to come up with a counter to my argument, I suspected.

"I ask only that you think it over and give me your answer in the morning," I said diplomatically. "My party is small. Only eight others, and myself. We would impose on your family as little as possible."

"We might make an exception for one," Zach said, "but never for eight. The location of our valley is a secret, and we aim to keep it that way."

He had inadvertently given me the leverage I needed. "Just me, then, with one packhorse for my art supplies and journals. How would that be?"

Ceran St. Vrain coughed. "I am not so sure Augustus Trevor will like the idea."

"Do you have any objection to him and the rest of my men waiting here at the trading post until I return?"

"None at all."

I smiled at Zach. "What do you say?"

"You gave me until morning to decide."

"I promise not to reveal where your valley is," I said. "I assure you I can be the soul of discretion."

"You won't be able to show anyone even if you wanted to," Zach said. "I intend to blindfold you when the time is right."

I did not relish riding in the mountain under such a handicap. "Is that really necessary?"

"It is if you want to come. But don't worry. I'll watch out for you until we get there."

I had him then, even if he did not realize it. "Whatever you deem best. All I ask is to be treated fairly."

"That is all I have ever wanted out of life," Zach said quietly. "But thanks to an accident of birth, most folks I meet either want to kick my teeth in or else want nothing to do with me."

"I would be honored to be considered your friend."

Zach King looked me in the eyes. "Very well. I will take you. But don't blame me if you live to regret it."

Chapter Five

True to Ceran St. Vrain's prediction, Augustus Trevor was not pleased. "I refuse to let you go. It is too dangerous."

"In case you have forgotten," I responded, "I hired you, not the other way around. I make the decisions. You must abide by them."

"But this is Zachary King we are talking about. He is a killer many times over. The worst ever, some folks say."

"Exaggerations, Mr. Trevor. Wild exaggerations."

Trevor shook his head. "I wish you would give it more thought. You will be completely on your own. I have never been to King Valley, and I don't know anyone who has. They say it is so well hidden, finding it is impossible."

"Zach King knows how to get there," I said dryly.

"Make light of it all you want. But I beg you to reconsider. I will worry myself sick until you get back."

"You are a good man, Augustus."

The scout sighed. "I could just shoot you."

He did not understand why I laughed so hard.

* * *

The next morning broke clear and crisp. I hurriedly dressed and went out to the square to await Zach King. Few others were out and about. One of the Bent brothers was opening shutters. He waved to me, and I waved back, then drifted toward the stable. I had no purpose other than killing time.

The stable doors were open. But then, they always were. There was no need to close and bar them when the stable was surrounded by high adobe walls, a sentry was always posted at the gate, and more men manned the ramparts.

I was almost to the shadowy entrance when several shapes materialized in its depths. Out came the three people I least desired to run into.

Jess Hook was carrying a half-empty whiskey bottle. He took a long swig and wiped his mouth with his sleeve. Passing the bottle to his brother, he spotted me. His face split into a vicious grin, and he came toward me, walking unsteadily. "Well, well, well. Look at what we have here. It's the fancy gent who thinks he's better'n everyone."

"I don't want trouble, Mr. Hook," I said. His brother and the other one, Cutter, stared at me with ill-concealed resentment. That they disliked me so intensely without real cause mystified me.

"Well, you have got trouble," Jess Hook said.

The smart thing for me to do was to walk away, but I was still smarting over their treatment of me the day before. "So much as raise a hand to me, and I will see to it that your actions are brought to the attention of the post's owners."

"I don't like to be threatened," Jess said. He did not have his rifle, but a pair of flintlocks were wedged under his belt.

"What you like or don't like is of no consequence," I

retorted. "If it had not been for Zach King, there is no telling what you would have done to me yesterday."

Cutter scowled and started toward me, his hands on his knives. "How about if I show you?" But as he went to pass Jess Hook, the latter gripped his arm.

"No."

"Let go. I don't like him. I don't like him one little bit."

"Not here," Jess Hook said, with a bob of his chin at the broad square. "We get the Bent boys or St. Vrain mad at us and they'll toss us out and won't ever let us back in."

Cutter's scowl faded but not the flinty glint in his dark eyes. "For now, then. But only for now."

I'd had about enough of their attitude. "Listen to yourselves. Grown men, and you go around blustering and posturing like ten-year-olds. No more, I say. You will leave me alone, here and elsewhere."

"Was that a threat, Big Words?" Jordy Hook said.

"I have eight men in my party," I informed them, "including Augustus Trevor, who I am sure you must have heard of, living on the frontier as you do. The next time you presume on my good graces, I will let Mr. Trevor and the rest deal with you."

"We know Trevor," Jess Hook said. "He's a tough one, but he's not us."

"What does that mean?" I demanded. My anger swelled when all they did was look at one another and smirk. "Are you saying that you are not afraid to tangle with Trevor? Then how about Zach King?"

"King?" Jess Hook repeated.

"He made you back down yesterday," I gloated. "And soon I expect to leave with him for the valley where he and his family live. I will be in his company for weeks." My intent was to show them that if they persisted in imposing on my good nature, they might have to answer to the most widely feared man on the frontier.

"He is taking you to King Valley?" Jess Hook asked in considerable surprise. "No one knows where it is except the Kings and that old goat Shakespeare Mc-Nair."

"So I have been told," I said.

"Folks say there's a reason the Kings keep it a secret," Jess went on. "They say the Kings found gold, and they're afraid that if words gets out, their valley will be overrun."

This was news to me. "I wouldn't know anything about any gold. My only interest is the wildlife."

"What is it you call yourself again?"

"A naturalist."

"And you expect us to believe you're more interested in critters than being rich?" Jess Hook laughed. "Mister, one of us is pulling the other's leg, and it ain't me."

"Believe what you will, but leave me be." I pivoted on my heel and strode off. I was simmering inside. I tried to tell myself that I shouldn't let three crude louts upset me so much. I was halfway to the trading post when I was hailed, and I promptly forgot about the unsavory trio in the excitement of seeing the man who had cowed them. I hurried to meet him. "Good morning. I have been waiting for you. I hope you haven't changed your mind."

Zach King placed the stock of his rifle on the ground and leaned on it. "I was up most of the night thanks to you. But when I give my word, I keep it."

"You lost sleep over taking me to your valley?"

"I wish my pa was here. It is his decision to make, not mine."

I was perplexed. "You are a grown man. Surely you can make up your own mind."

"It's not that," Zach said. "I told you. We like our privacy. If word of how to find our valley ever got out, we would have hunters and trappers and you-name-it paying us a visit every time we turned around."

"And gold seekers," I mentioned. "Rumor has it your family made a rich strike."

"I've heard that nonsense," Zach said. "It started when Shakespeare paid for some supplies with a nugget he found years ago. Tongues commenced to wag, and pretty soon that nugget turned into a vein of pure gold somewhere in our valley. We tell people it's not true, but they think we're lying." He let out a long sigh. "When folks get silly notions like that into their heads, nothing you can say will change their minds."

"What was it you said to Cutter yesterday? Oh, yes, now I remember," I said. "'Stupid is as stupid does.'"

"Exactly." Zach smiled.

"To get back to the issue at hand," I said. "Don't keep me in suspense. When do we head out?"

With obvious reluctance, Zach said, "First you must agree to the conditions."

"I already said you can blindfold me. What else is there?"

"You will do as I say at all times. No arguments. Ever. When it comes time to blindfold you, if I catch you trying to peek from under it, we go our separate ways. Once we reach the valley, you are not to leave it for any reason until you are done doing whatever it is you do. Then me or one of the others will escort you out. Blindfolded, of course."

"Of course," I said. "Your requests seem reasonable enough."

"They are not requests," Zach warned. "If, at any

time, I suspect you are up to no good, I will take whatever steps are called for." He studied me. "I hope to God you are sincere. If this is a trick, if later you bring others to our valley, I will kill you."

"Just like that?" I bantered, and snapped my fingers.

"Just like that," Zach King said.

Something in his tone persuaded me I should take him seriously. "It's no trick. I promise. So how soon do we leave?"

"I have some supplies to buy," Zach replied. "We will head out about two this afternoon."

"I'll be ready."

"Just so you understand," Zach said, and pointed to the west. "You have never been in the mountains. You have no idea what it's like. I will do my best, but I can't promise that you will make it back alive."

"Honestly," I said with a grin. "It won't work. You can't scare me into changing my mind."

"You don't get it," Zach responded. "You think I am making much ado about nothing, as Shakespeare McNair would say. But the plain truth is that in the wild it is do or die. Nature does not play favorites. A mistake can cost you your life."

"You have managed well enough," I said. "You and your entire family. Including a younger sister, I hear." I chuckled. "If she manages, so can I."

"My sister and I were raised in the wilderness. We know all the animals and their ways. We know the plants and the trees. We can read the land, the weather and the stars. We never get lost. Can you say the same?"

"The sun rises in the east and sets in the west," I glibly responded. "How hard can it be?"

"That's not what I meant." Again Zach sighed. "You will find out for yourself soon enough. Be sure to bring a rifle and two pistols and a water skin if you have one."

"I thank you from the bottom of my heart."

The next several hours went by in a rush. Before I knew it, it was noon, and I sat down to eat with Trevor and Jeffers and the rest. The scout sought to talk me out of going, but I was immune to his entreaties. Finally I held up my hand.

"Enough. I appreciate your concern. I truly do. But I have made up my mind. You are to wait here until I return. I will pay you the same as I would if we were on the trail."

"If you insist," the scout said. "But mark my words. You will regret your decision."

"Zach King was right," I teased. "Much ado about nothing."

At ten minutes until two, I was at the gate on my horse, a rifle in one hand and the lead rope to the pack horse in the other. I had not seen Zach since morning and half feared he had changed his mind and slipped away without my noticing. Then he approached leading his mount and pack animal.

Ceran St. Vrain was at his side.

I suppose I was beaming like an idiot because they looked at each other and Zach King shook his head.

"I came to see you off," St. Vrain said. "Unless I can prevail on you to change your mind."

"You, too?" I accused.

"Augustus Trevor came to see me," St. Vrain revealed. "He begged me to use whatever small influence I might have to convince you that you are making a mistake."

"The nerve," I said. It seemed to me that everyone thought I was a total imcompetent.

"You are determined to go through with this, aren't you?"

"Need you ask?"

"You are a grown man," St. Vrain said. "But there is a saying out here that you should give some thought to." He paused. "You can talk sense to a smart man but not to a fool."

"That was harsh," I said.

"Mr. Parker, I flatter myself that I know the frontier better than most. I can not stress the perils enough. So far you have had it remarkably easy. Oh, yes, I heard about the stampede, but in general your prairie crossing was free of mishaps, thanks in large measure to Augustus Trevor." St. Vrain indicated the gate. "Once you go through there, you take your life in your hands. Zach, here, will do his best to keep you alive, but there is only so much he can do, and I would hate for—"

I held up my hand. "Enough."

"I beg your pardon?"

"No more," I declared. "As you pointed out, I am a grown man. It is my decision to make, and I have made it. Nothing you or anyone else can say will change my mind."

"Very well then," St. Vrain said stiffly.

"Hear me out," I went on. "I am a naturalist. My passion is life in all its variety. I collect specimens. I paint animals and flowers and trees. The Rockies are a treasure trove for those in my profession. Only two other naturalists that I know of have been there before me. The opportunities are boundless. If I were to back out, I might as well shovel manure for a living."

"I will not argue with such eloquence," St. Vrain said. "May you find all that you are looking for, and may the Almighty in His omniscience spare you from your folly."

I thanked him, we shook hands, and he gave the order to have the gate opened. Zach King had been strangely silent during our exchange, and I said to him, "What? No comments to add?"

"Since you asked, there is another expression we have in these parts." Zach looked at me. "Every coon digs his own grave."

On that note I followed him out of the trading post and off into the dark heart of the unknown.

Chapter Six

Ah! The sweet intoxicating joy of the moment when we reached the foothills! I was practically giddy with excitement.

My powers of description fail me when it comes to describing the Rockies. Compared to them, the mountains of the East are no more than glorified bumps. The Rockies tower *miles* into the atmosphere. Some peaks, Zach King informed me, are as much as three miles high, if not more. To behold them staggers the mind. They dwarf everything and fill a man with the sense that in the scheme of creation he is pitifully tiny. At the same time, their majesty, their grandeur, their imposing sweep, inspire the soul to new heights. I am no poet, but I swear to you that the effect was so overpowering, I was tempted to try my hand at it.

My companion was not nearly as enamored. He rode alertly, his Hawken across the saddle in front of him. Again and again he shifted to look back. I checked behind us a few times but saw nothing to account for his interest.

We were well up into the foothills when Zach twisted in the saddle yet again, compelling me to ask, "Why do you keep doing that?"

"We're being followed."

"What? The devil you say!" I turned and stared long and hard. "I don't see anyone."

"He is back there."

"It is just one man?" For a moment I was worried it might be the Hook brothers and Cutter.

"One is too many. He's been following us all afternoon. You'll see for yourself once the sun goes down unless he makes a cold camp."

We stopped for the night on the crown of a hill. Zach picked the spot, I divined, for the view it gave of the surrounding countryside. At his bidding I gathered firewood. As he opened his possibles bag and took out a fire steel and flint, I could not help asking, "Is building a fire wise? It will tell our shadow where we are."

"He already knows. For us not to have one might make him suspect we know he is back there."

"What do you intend to do about it?"

"Find out who it is."

"How?"

Zach did not answer. I was to learn that was a habit of his when he did not care to divulge his intentions.

"We didn't shoot game for the supper pot. What will we eat?"

"I have plenty of jerky and pemmican. We won't go hungry."

Jerky, I was familiar with; I ate a lot of it while crossing the prairie. Pemmican, however, was new to me. It seems that it is a staple of the Indians. They dry buffalo meat, grind it until the consistency resembles flour, then mix it with fat and berries. Zach King kept his in a beaded bag he called a parfleche, apparently his mother's handiwork. Her craftsmanship was superb.

We were about done eating when Zach pointed and said, "Our shadow is filling his belly, too."

Sure enough, a tiny orange tongue licked at the darkness lower down. Even as I set eyes on it, the light blinked out, only to reappear a few seconds later. Then, to my amazement, it blinked out and reappeared a second time. "What in the world?"

"He camped in trees to hide his fire," Zach said. "But when the wind blows, we catch a glimpse of it."

"Who can it be?" I wondered.

"You don't know?"

The accusation in his voice brought my head around. "What are you suggesting? That I had one of my party follow us? To what end?"

"A lot of people would like to know where King Valley is."

I was offended. "I agreed to the conditions you set down, and I will abide by them."

Zach shrugged. "We will find out tomorrow."

"What are you saying?"

"That our shadow is in for a surprise." Zach's mouth curled in a grin that did not bode well for whoever was back there.

Need I say I had trouble falling asleep? It occurred to me that Zach might be right and I could be wrong through no fault of my own. I would not put it past Augustus Trevor to follow us despite my express wishes, or to have Jeffers or one of the others do so. He missed his calling being a scout; he should hire out as a nursemaid.

Eventually, though, slumber claimed me. I was so tired I slept straight through until I awoke to the shake of a hand on my shoulder.

Stars still ruled the firmament. To the east a golden glow framed the horizon. The sun would rise in half an hour, or thereabouts.

"You like getting an early start, I take it," I grumbled.

"We have a long way to go," Zach said.

I had not thought to ask, but I did so now. "How long will this trip take, anyhow?"

"Twelve to fourteen days, depending."

"On what?"

"Whether everything goes well." Zach held out some pemmican and I accepted.

"Don't construe this the wrong way," I said, "but you have a cynical nature. You always expect the worst."

"I see things as they are, not as I would like them to be."

"Do I detect criticism?" I bit into the pemmican and chewed with relish. It truly was delicious. I could understand why Indians liked it so much.

"Life is not the rainbow you make it out to be," Zach said. "Life is blood and guts and claws and fangs. Life is an arrow in the back, a bullet to the brain. Life is the Piegans staking you out and peeling the skin from your body. Life is the Bloods digging your eyeballs from their sockets and cutting off your ears."

"Dear Lord. They do that?"

"My pa and I once came across a trapper who had no eyes, no nose, no tongue. No fingers or toes, either. He still had his manhood, but it had been chopped off and stuffed in his mouth."

I stopped chewing. My stomach was churning.

"Down Santa Fe way, the Apaches struck a bunch of freight wagons. When we happened by, everyone was dead. I was only a boy at the time, and the thing I remember most is a freighter who had been tied upside down to a wagon wheel."

"Why upside down?" I asked despite myself.

"The Apaches lit a fire under his head and baked his brains. He was the lucky one. Some of the other freighters took hours to die."

I had the impression this young man had witnessed an incredible amount of violence in his life. "Forgive me if I overstep myself, but I've heard that you have taken a few lives, yourself."

Zach did not rise to the bait.

"Forgive me again, but how old were you when you killed your first man?" I justified my prying by telling myself that I was seeking insight into his character.

"What do you want to know for? So you can scribble it in that book you are always writing in."

"It's my journal," I explained. "An account of my experiences. When I return to the States, I will combine what I have written with my paintings and sketches to broaden the scope of our understanding of the West."

"You intend to tell the whole world I am bloodthirsty?" Zach asked resentfully.

"Only if you are. I strive to be factual. When I write about you, I will present you as you are."

"Don't," Zach said.

"Don't what?"

"Write about my family if you have to, but leave me out. Too many people have heard about me as it is."

"How so?" I inquired, but he did not reply.

On that somewhat sour note our day began. We climbed steadily, hour after hour, winding along a game trail marked with deer tracks and occasional elk prints. We were so high up that when I glanced down at the prairie one last time, several antelope I spied were no bigger than ants.

I was more interested in the mountains. Before us

reared a spine of peaks, the Continental Divide. To the south was the Sangre de Cristo Range. To the north the Rockies extended clear into Canada.

Even in the summer the highest peaks were crowned white with snow. Their ivory mantles glistened in testament to their altitude.

Prime timber cloaked the slopes, spruce and pine and firs, the latter more common higher up. Here and there stands of aspens broke the monotony of the evergreens.

The woodland alternated with broad grassy tracts called parks. They were a special treat for me because they were rife with wildflowers; columbines, daisies, wild geraniums, buttercups and more. When we came upon some wild roses I asked Zach to stop so I could sketch them. He told me there were some in King Valley, and we could not afford the delay.

No sooner did we reach the next belt of woodland, though, than he drew rein and announced, "We will stop here a spell."

"What for?"

"So whoever is following us can catch up." Zach swung down and led his horses farther into the woods.

More than mildly irritated, I did likewise. "We have time for this, but we could not spare the time for me to sketch those roses?"

"Roses won't slit our throats while we sleep." Zach looped the reins and the lead rope around separate saplings, hefted his rifle, and retraced his steps to the tree line.

"Do you know what your problem is?" I asked when I caught up with him. "You think the whole world is out to get you."

"Tell it to that freighter I told you about," Zach responded, and hunkered by a bole.

"I admit man's inhumanity to man is boundless. But that is hardly cause to distrust everyone."

"Say what you want," Zach said. "I still have my hair."

How can you dispute logic like that? I settled down to wait, opened my bag and took out my journal.

Half an hour went by. An hour. I was about ready to insist we move on when Zach King whispered, "Stay down and don't make a sound."

I gazed across the park and my breath caught in my throat.

A horse and rider were at the edge of the trees. At least, so I assumed; they were in the shadow of a tall spruce, and I could not see them clearly. Then the horse moved into the open.

"What in the world?" I blurted.

"Hush," Zach said.

It was uncalled for. The horse was too far away to hear me. I opened my mouth to say as much but decided not to.

The horse came toward us. A saddle was on its back, and reins dangled. But no one was in the saddle. No one was holding those reins.

"Where can its owner be?" I whispered.

"Maybe in the trees with a rifle," Zach answered, "waiting for us to show ourselves so he can pick us off."

I had not thought of that. A devilish ruse, if that was the case. The horse acted skittish, and stopped often to raise its head and prick its ears. When it was twenty feet away, I looked at Zach, half expecting him to rush out to grab the reins. But he didn't move.

The animal, a splendid sorrel, came closer.

Zach stood and stepped from behind the tree. Holding out a hand, he smiled and said softly, "Here, boy."

The horse stopped. It stamped a hoof, but it did not run off.

"Don't be afraid," Zach said. "I won't hurt you."

I thought he was saying that to soothe the animal's nerves. It advanced, and I noticed, with a start, a bright red splotch on the saddle. "Blood!" I blurted.

The sorrel glanced at me and stood poised for flight.

"Nice and easy," Zach cautioned. "We don't want it to run off." He moved nearer, saying to the sorrel, "Don't be scared, big fella. He's friendly and so am I."

He had a way with animals.

That sorrel let him walk right up to it and take hold of the reins. Patting its neck, Zach said, "There, now. We'll look after you."

I was surprised. He gave me the impression I was more of a nuisance than anything else. Moving slowly so as not to scare the sorrel, I joined him.

"What do you make of it?" I asked.

The red splotch I had noticed was not the only one. There were more, on the saddle and on the horse, itself. The largest was behind the saddle. Scarlet lines streaked the animal's sides and rear legs. Whoever the rider was, he had lost an awful lot of blood.

Zach touched a splotch and held his fingers so I could see the tips weren't red. The blood was dry. "Whatever happened, happened hours ago. About daybreak, I would say."

"Who could it have been?" I asked in puzzlement. "And what could have happened to them?"

He shrugged.

"Why did the horse follow us?"

"Maybe because it had our scent. Maybe because it is used to human company." Zach paused. "Is it one of yours?"

"What? Heavens, no. I have never seen it before."

Taking the reins, Zach led the sorrel into the woods. "We'll add it to our string and take it with us."

"You haven't said what you think," I prompted, eager to get his opinion.

Zach twisted and stared intently at the far end of the park. "I think we'd better light a shuck."

Chapter Seven

The next two days were an ordeal and then some. Zach pushed us and our animals to the point of exhaustion. It did not help that rather than stick to open areas where the going was easier, he deliberately chose the most difficult terrain—the thickest timber, the steepest slopes. And to make matters worse, we never went more than a mile or two in any one direction; we would ride north, then west, then south, then west again.

I understood why. He suspected we were still being followed, and he wanted to shake whoever was following us. But we had five horses now, and they left plenty of sign of our passing.

Along about late afternoon of the second day, I piped up with, "This is pointless. A ten-year-old could track us."

"Not after tomorrow," Zach said.

"Our horses are going to sprout wings and fly?"

"Would that they could," Zach replied. "But we will do the next best thing."

He did not elaborate.

We pushed on until dark and made a cold camp. I missed not having a fire and dearly yearned for a cup or three of piping hot coffee. But Zach said the fire would give us away.

"We could be doing all this for nothing," I pointed out. "Whoever killed that man might not even be after us."

"Better cautious than dead."

I was tempted to say his paranoia had gotten the better of him, but then I remembered the blood on the sorrel.

The next day we worked our way up a mountain until we were above the timber line. The climb was arduous. Deadfalls were everywhere, and had to be skirted. Narrow ravines necessitated constant detours. I did not think much of his choice of routes. I thought even less when he led us toward a wide slope littered with small stones. We were right out in the open, leaving tracks as plain as could be.

Zach drew rein and bobbed his chin. "Talus," he said, as if that should mean something.

"Is that good or bad?" I had never heard the term.

"Stay close. Have your horse step exactly where mine does." Zach reined to the left and tugged on the lead rope.

His reasoning escaped me, but I did as he wanted. It took us over half an hour to reach the south side of the mountain. Here the slope was bare except for a sprinkling of scrub vegetation. I figured he would keep on going to the other side of the mountain, but he reined to the right and headed for the top.

"I hope you know what you are doing," I remarked.

The pinnacle was a stark spine of solid rock, but we did not climb that high. A quarter of a mile below the summit, Zach unexpectedly stopped and said, "Wait here." He handed me his lead rope.

I was at a loss. There seemed to be no purpose to

his actions. I watched as he rode along the base of the spine until he was directly above the slope strewn with small stones. He dismounted near a cluster of boulders. For a while he stood contemplating the slope, then he stepped to a boulder as big as a wash-basin. It was perched on the very lip of the incline. He put his shoulder to it, dug in his heels, and strained.

I had to marvel at his strength. I doubted I could move that boulder, but he did. Inch by begrudging inch it gave way, until, with a loud crash, it went tumbling down the stone-covered slope.

I was not prepared for what happened next.

In my ignorance I assumed the slope was solid earth. But it was no such thing. For as the boulder rolled, it dislodged not only those small stones, but the earth underneath as well. Rapidly gaining momentum and mass, the talus, as Zach had called it, cascaded down the mountain, a river of dirt and rock that would have crushed any living thing in its path.

A great rumble rose and echoed off nearby peaks. It reminded me of the buffalo stampede.

The talus crashed into the timber. Entire trees were uprooted, limbs were snapped like twigs. Scores of trees disappeared, buried in the twinkling of an eye.

I was in awe of the devastation.

Zach came riding back with a smile on his face. "Not bad, if I say so myself."

"Congratulations," I said dryly. "You have wiped out half the mountain."

"And our tracks."

Sometimes I wonder about the gray matter between my ears. "If anyone is following us, they will never find us now!" I exulted.

"A good tracker could pick up our trail again, but that will take some time." Zach motioned at the tendrils of dust rising from the broad expanse of displaced terra firma.

I had to hand it to my young companion. He was resourceful in the extreme. Presently, as we wound down the other side the mountain, he resorted to another of the wily tricks he had up his buckskin sleeves.

A stream bisected our course, flowing out of the northwest and off to the southeast. As with many mountain waterways it was fast flowing but shallow. Zach promptly reined into the water and started upstream, riding in the very middle. He beckoned for me to imitate him.

Yet another stroke of brilliance. Most of our tracks were washed away by the strong current.

"You think of everything," I complimented him.

"Repeat that when you meet my sister," Zach said. "She says my head and a tree stump have a lot in common."

The affection in his tone was undeniable. "I gather you love your family very much."

He glanced sharply back at me. "Why wouldn't I? Don't you care for yours?"

If he only knew. My father ran a dry goods business. He had expected me to take it over once he was too old to work. My decision to become a naturalist appalled him. He could never understand my fascination with the outdoors, or how deeply I disliked doing account books and juggling figures in my head. He shocked me one day by giving me an ultimatum: either give up my silly interest in biology or be banished from home until I came to my senses.

We had not seen each other in seven years.

My mother, bless her, approved of my work, but she was too timid to stand up to my father and tell him that. Whatever he told her to do, she did, even if she was against doing it. Tears moistened her eyes the day I left. She hugged me and kissed me, then stepped back to my father's side.

I have a brother, but he and I are as different as day and night. He, too, has no interest in dry goods. He would rather spend his days loafing and his nights in taverns and saloons. But my father did not banish Edward as he did me. Ed has always been his favorite. Sour grapes on my part, you might say, but you would be mistaken. I am simply mentioning the facts.

So, yes, while I did care for my family, there were limits to my caring. Unlike Zach King, my affection was tempered by their treatment of me. It is hard to give unconditional love to someone whose own love for you is conditioned by whether you do as they want you to do.

"You are a lucky man, Zach King," I remarked.

He laughed bitterly. "To be born a halfbreed is hardly what I would call a stroke of luck."

"You never stop thinking about that, do you?"

"When I was seven my father took me to a rendezvous. This was back in the days when the beaver trade was at its height. I was wandering around, looking at the goods and weapons and whatnot for sale, and I bumped into a trapper. He was swilling from a jug, and when I bumped him, he spilled some down his chin. I told him I was sorry." Zach paused. "He said, 'Watch where you are going, you breed gnat.' And then he spat on me."

"Oh my. What did you do?"

"What could I do? I was only a boy. I turned to go when suddenly Uncle Shakespeare was there. He had heard what the man said, and he walked right up and broke the man's jaw with the butt of his rifle."

"Uncle Shakespeare? You called him that before. Is McNair related to your father?"

"No. But we have always called him our uncle. He is part of our family, blood ties or not."

"I look forward to meeting him."

After a few miles Zach reined out of the stream. We pushed on, generally northwest, surrounded by the most glorious mountains imaginable. The roof of the continent, the Rockies have been called, and the title is apt. Near bottomless gorges, canyons whose walls were streaked with glistening quartz, phalanxes of firs and colorful stands of aspens. So much to drink in, a man could not absorb it all.

Then there were the animals. Black-tailed deer far larger than their white-tailed low-country cousins. Regal elk, each as big as a horse. Mountain sheep, white spots on the high cliffs. Black bears, which usually left people alone, and grizzly bears, which often didn't.

The lesser animals were of no less interest to me.

Rabbits were not as plentiful as on the prairie, but those we saw were bigger. Squirrels scolded us from the safety of high branches. At one juncture, we were crossing a slope when I distinctly heard someone whistle. I cast about but saw no one. The whistle was repeated, so I asked Zach who the deuce was whistling at us. He laughed, and drew rein. In a bit he pointed up the mountain.

I spied a creature of the rodent variety, about two feet in length with brown fur, perched on its hind legs and staring down at us. It suddenly let out a piercing whistle and vanished from view.

"A marmot," Zach explained. "That whistle is their danger signal. They live in burrows much like prairie dogs."

Nor were they the only ones. Two days later, toward evening, we had stopped for the day and Zach was skinning a rabbit he had shot. I wandered off with my pad to sketch and spotted an earthen den of some sort higher up. I investigated. The hole was bigger than any I had yet seen, and I was curious as to the inhabitant. I did not stay curious long. For as I bent to peer into the hole, out of it rushed the irate tenant, snarling and bristling and snapping at my legs. I barely leaped back in time.

Zach heard the racket and came on the run, and had another good laugh at my expense. "A badger," he confirmed my surmise. "I can shoot it if you want the hide."

"Heavens, no."

The badger hissed, its back to the mound of dirt, its dark eyes mirrors of ferocity. Thick bodied, with short legs, its mouth was rimmed with razor-sharp teeth. I particularly admired the white stripe that ran down its broad back, and the white markings on its face. "Do you suppose we could catch it so I can paint it?" I envisioned containing it in a cage. We could build one of tree limbs.

"I know a Shoshone who lost two fingers to a badger," Zach mentioned. "Have you looked in its mouth?"

I frowned in disappointment. I could always paint by memory, of course, but having the animal before me was infinitely better for capturing the small details my memory might miss.

"There are badgers in our valley," Zach said. "I will give it some thought, and when we get there, we will try."

I had the impression he was growing more and more anxious to reach his home. Dunce that I am, I kept forgetting an important fact. "You miss your wife, don't you?"

Zach had started to back away from the badger. "What brought that up?"

"Your mention of your valley," I said, easing backward. I was not looking at the badger but at him. "It is nothing to be embarrassed about. If I had a wife, I would—"

"Look out!" Zach shouted.

A searing pain shot up my left leg and I was bowled over. The only thing I can compare it to is being tackled by my brother when we were younger and would roughhouse. The pain was terrible. I came down on my back and instinctively reached for my hurt leg. I almost lost fingers. A snap of the badger's teeth missed my hand by a whisker. I sought to scramble back out of its reach, but with a swift lunge it was on me again, its teeth shearing into my right shin this time, ripping through cloth and skin. I am afraid I cried out.

Then Zach was there, looming with his Hawken to his shoulder, taking quick aim.

"Don't kill it!" I yelled. The animal was only defending its den. The fault was mine; I had been careless.

Zach looked at me in disbelief.

The badger gave my leg a hard shake, and I gritted my teeth against the agony. I kicked at it with my other leg to try and drive him off me but my kick had no effect other than to make the badger madder than it already was.

Just then Zach reversed his hold on his rifle and raised it overhead to bring the hardwood stock smashing down.

"No! You might hurt it!"

Under different circumstances, Zach's expression

would have been comical. "Are you loco?" he responded in amazement.

The badger let go.

I flung myself backward, my elbows digging into the ground. I thought the badger would let me go, but I was wrong.

The creature pounced, moving incredibly fast for its bulk, and bit at my right wrist. Its teeth caught my sleeve, not my arm, and it shook its blunt triangular head from side to side in a frenzy.

I tried to push it away, but it weighed upward of thirty pounds. A savage snarl rose from its throat. I went to push to my knees, when without warning the badger slammed into my chest, knocking me flat.

Before I could collect my wits, I was on my back again and the badger was on top of me, its glistening teeth spreading wide to tear at my throat.

Chapter Eight

Of all the ways to die, being slain by a badger has to qualify as unique.

I braced for the sensation of its fangs tearing my flesh and the warm gout of blood that would ensue. But suddenly the badger seemed to fly off me and swing around in midair. Then I saw that Zach had hold of its rear legs and had torn it off me. He released his hold, and the badger hit the ground with a thud and rolled.

I feared Zach had hurt it, but the animal was up in the blink of an eye. It snarled and hissed, then whirled and vanished down its hole with a speed that belied its size.

"Well," I said, for lack of anything better. Zach picked up his rifle and turned to me. "You saved my life. I thank you."

Zach simply stared.

"Say something," I prompted.

"You are an idiot."

"I beg your pardon?"

"You heard me," Zach said. "You nearly got yourself killed, and for what? To spare an animal that was out to kill you? If that's not being an idiot, I don't know what is."

"Really, now," I said, offended.

"Try that stunt with a grizzly or a mountain lion, and I will bury what is left of you and laugh when I do it."

"I would never get that close to either," I responded indignantly. "I am not entirely without common sense."

"A thimbleful isn't much to brag about." Zach squatted. "Let's take a look at you."

It was not as bad as it looked. My sleeve was ripped, but my wrist had been spared. Both shins were bloody and my pants torn, but the bites were not all that deep, and the bleeding had about stopped. "See?" I said, wincing. "I'll live. There was no call to kill it."

Zach was bent over my right leg, examining the wound. "I don't like the looks of this one."

"I will be in pain for a few days, but I will be fine," I said. "It is not as if a couple of bites will kill me."

"That's just it," Zach said. "They can."

"I have been bitten before. It is nothing to get excited about."

"Maybe not back East where there are plenty of doctors to tend you. But out here"—Zach gestured to encompass the wilderness—"just about any wound can land you in the grave."

"Posh and poppycock," I declared.

Zach regarded me much as you might regard a wayward child. "Evidently no one ever told you."

"Told me what?" I was sure he was trying to put a scare into me for my insisting he spare the badger.

"About what kills more folks than anything else. It's not guns or bows or lances or knives. It's not claws or fangs or talons. It is the infection that sets in."

"You exaggerate, sir."

"For every man who dies of a bullet to the brain or the heart, nine more die from being shot in the leg or the arm. For every warrior who goes down from an arrow or a lance to a vital organ, nine more die from minor wounds. The cause is always the same. The blood turns foul." Zach indicated my shins. "I've seen worse bites than these, sure. But that's not the point. Even the smallest bite can become infected, and if it does, you're as good as dead."

He was so greatly in earnest that I grew alarmed. "You are serious? You are not pulling my leg?"

Zach surprised me by placing a hand on my shoulder. "I would never joke about a thing like this. We need to clean and bandage you, and pray to high heaven the rot in that badger's mouth did not get into your blood."

"The rot?" I repeated.

"All meat eaters have bits of rotting flesh between their teeth from the critters they have fed on. That's what mixes with your blood and turns it putrid."

Genuine fear washed through me. "I didn't realize," I said, my mouth going dry as the implications sank in.

"Most newcomers don't." Zach slipped an arm around me and assisted me in rising. He smiled in encouragement. "So long as you don't come down with a fever, you won't have anything to worry about."

All night I tossed and turned. I was so hot, I was caked with sweat. I told myself it was because of my blankets, and toward morning I cast them off.

Zach was up before the sun rose and immediately came to my side. He saw I was awake. "How are you feeling?" he asked, pressing a palm to my brow.

"Tired, but otherwise fine."

"You have a fever."

"That doesn't necessarily mean I am infected," I said. But I knew. I was just being pigheaded.

Zach went to one of his parfleches and rummaged inside. "My mother packed some herbs for me. She has considerable skill as a healer."

"Herbs?" I said skeptically.

"Indians have cures for all sorts of ailments. Pine gum for boils. Sagebrush leaves for indigestion. Elderberry roots for inflammation." Zach brought out a packet tied with twine and set it down. "A lot of their cures, the white man doesn't know about."

"Are there herbs in there that will help me?"

Zach began undoing the twine. "What the Shoshones call *unda vich quana*. It will fight the infection. Then there is a tea I can make to bring down your fever."

"You are going to a lot of trouble on my account," I remarked.

"Would you rather die?"

All that day I lay feverish and sweating. Zach applied poultices to my shins and made me drink a cup of tea every hour or so. I felt awful, slowing us up this way, but it could not be helped. I was too weak to ride.

That night I was worse. I hardly remember any of it except that I was constantly sweating and constantly shivering. How you can be hot and cold at the same time is a mystery, but I was. By morning I was so helpless, Zach had to tilt a tin cup to my lips to get the tea into me.

About the middle of the afternoon the fever broke. I became aware of the blue of the sky and white pillowy clouds and of the breeze on my face. I smelled my own sweat and longed for a bath. Licking my lips, I turned my head.

Zach was nowhere to be seen.

Panicked, I tried to rise on my elbows but couldn't. For a few wild moments I feared he had deserted me. Yes, I should have known better. He had already demonstrated he was not the ogre he was reputed to be.

I licked my dry lips and croaked, "Zach? Zach? Where are you?" When there was no answer, my panic climbed. I struggled to sit up and was afflicted with dizziness. Then a shadow fell across me. I gave a violent start, convinced some beast had found me.

"What in the world is all the fuss about?"

I looked up. Zach had a small doe over his shoulder and was regarding me in puzzlement. "Where have you been?" I said.

"Off hunting." Zach gave the body a thump. "You need meat, and a lot of it, to build your strength."

I almost burst into tears.

"Are you all right?" Zach dropped the deer and knelt beside me. "I checked you earlier and would have sworn we beat the fever."

"Why are you doing all this for me?" I foolishly asked.

Zach shrugged. "You need help."

"But you hardly know me. And gossip has it that you hate whites, yet here you are, doctoring a white man."

Chuckling, Zach replied, "My wife is white, and I sure don't hate her. My father is white, and so is Shakespeare McNair, and they are two of the most decent men I know." He sobered and said, "It is not whites I hate, it is white *bigots*. Or red bigots. Or any kind of bigot."

"I will be forever in your debt. Anything you ever want of me, you have only to ask."

"There is one thing."

"Name it and I will do it," I pledged.

"Whatever you do, don't take it into your head to paint a griz. If a badger can do this to you, just think what a bear would do."

I blinked and laughed and could not stop. Perhaps it was an emotional release. But I laughed as if his little joke was the funniest I ever heard. I laughed until my ribs ached, and just when my mirth subsided, he made another comment.

"Stick to chipmunks and squirrels and you should be safe."

I convulsed anew.

"Or how about insects and birds? I think butterflies and wrens would be best. They are about as harmless as anything gets."

"Please," I begged between gasps. "I'm ready to split a gut." But the laughter did me good in that it restored some of my vitality, to the point where I could sit up unaided. I suspect he made me laugh for that express purpose.

Strange to relate, but whatever barrier had existed between us was gone. I thought of him as a friend, and I flatter myself that he began to think the same of me. He was more talkative thereafter, and I detected none of the wariness that was so much a part of his nature. He had accepted me, and I accepted him.

I wanted to head out the next morning, but Zach wouldn't hear of it. He claimed I needed a day to rest, and I did not object too strenuously.

That evening we were seated by the fire eating roasted venison when Zach remarked, "I've been thinking about that horse."

There are moments when I wonder if I have a brain. This was one of them. "What horse?"

"The one with the blood. The one I have been leading around the past couple of days."

"Oh." The truth was, in my delirium I had forgotten about it. I glanced at where the animals were picketed.

"I've seen that sorrel before," Zach said, and tore off a strip of venison with his teeth.

"You have? Where?"

"In a corral at Bent's Fort."

"You are certain? Who did it belong to?" As I recalled, the fort had two large inside corrals, one at the north end of the post and the other on the west side. Between them, they could hold over three hundred horses, mules and oxen.

"The Bent brothers," Zach said. "They have stock for trade and sale, and sometimes they rent horses out for short spells."

"So the Bents could have sold or traded it to practically anyone?"

"Well, we know it wasn't an Indian," Zach said with his mouth full, and lustily chewing.

"We do?"

"The saddle," Zach said. "Indians don't much like white saddles. They use their own or ride bareback." He chewed some more. "No, I think it was a white man, but then that doesn't explain the bedroll and the packs."

"There weren't any."

"Exactly. And white men don't go anywhere without their bedroll and supplies."

I had not considered that. It added to the mystery.

Three days of travel went by. By then we were deep in the mountains. I came to appreciate why much of the Rockies were unexplored. Except for the intrepid trappers of a generation ago, few white men had ever penetrated this far in among the towering peaks.

Zach filled my head with facts about the land and the wildlife. I learned, for instance, that many of the streams only flowed during the winter and spring, that in the summer much that was green became parched and brown. And a lot of the water that did flow came from runoff from the snow high up. Rain was a relative rarity except in the summer when fierce thunderstorms broke out.

I was particularly interested in the habits of the animals, and in that Zach did not disappoint. He was a font of information. I surmised that he had been a keen student of nature while growing up. When I made a comment in that regard, he looked at me and said he had never thought of it that way. He had learned what he had to in order to survive. I added that in my opinion, he would make an excellent guide for others who might want to venture into the mountains.

Zach mentioned that whites were coming to the Rockies in greater numbers of late. It was the main reason his father had decided to move deeper in. He alluded to half a dozen homesteads scattered along the foothills.

I replied that it would not be long before whites did to the Rocky Mountains as they had done to the Appalachians in the East. "No barrier, not even the Rockies, can stop the tide of western expansion," I said, parroting what I had read in many newspapers. "Our Manifest Destiny will not be denied."

"Leave it to white men to think that multiplying like rabbits makes them special."

He grinned as he said it, but I detected an undertone of bitterness. He did not want to see the mountains overrun, and I can't say as I blame him. Man—and when I say that I mean humanity in general, men and women combined—insists on turning wilderness into farmland and filling it with towns and cities, wiping out the wild in favor of the tame and the safe.

That is what it was all about: living safe. People did not want to worry about being eaten by a grizzly whenever they stepped out their door.

This was impressed on me the very next day.

We stopped to rest the horses at noon. I spotted a woodpecker off in the woods, and taking my sketchbook, I hurried to catch it on paper before it flew off. It was the first of its kind I had seen, and I was so excited, I left my rifle behind. I lost sight of the woodpecker but continued toward where I had seen it last. I moved quietly, in order not to startle it into flight should I suddenly come upon it.

I was so intent on finding the woodpecker that I paid no attention to the woods around me, an oversight I regretted when the undergrowth abruptly crackled to the passage of an immense form, and into the open lumbered a flesh-and-blood behemoth.

Chapter Nine

Another interesting fact Zach King had taught me, a fact few whites were aware of, was that there were two kinds of buffalo, not just one. Most people were familiar with the vast herds that grazed the plains, but few had ever heard that prairie buffalo had shaggier cousins who preferred mountain forests to grassland.

And here I was, face-to-face with one.

When I say it was a behemoth I do not exaggerate. It stood six feet at the shoulder and was over ten feet in length. In color it was a dark brown bordering on black. Its coat was, as I noted, shaggy, the long hairs thick and matted. I would say this one weighed well over a thousand pounds. It had a short tail with a tuft at the end, which constantly twitched, and large, dark hooves. But what impressed me the most were its striking hump, its broad head, and especially the pair of black horns that curved like scythes.

I froze, transfixed with amazement and awe.

The buffalo stared a few moments, then snorted and pawed the ground as if about to charge.

My awe was replaced by fear. I had my pistols, but

they were a puny defense. Should it attack, it would be on me before I could draw and shoot. I wanted to wilt into the earth.

Movement behind the buffalo warned me there were others. I had stumbled on a small herd. The bull confronting me was protecting the others.

I did not know what to do. My instinct was to flee, but Zach had told me never to run, that to take flight nearly always provoked an animal into giving chase. But he had been talking about meat eaters at the time. I wondered if the same applied to buffalo.

The bull snorted again, and repeated its gouging of the earth with its great dark hoove.

I thought that if I stayed stock-still it would lose interest and leave, but instead it took a step toward me and rumbled deep in its massive chest, a prelude, for all I knew, to rushing me.

Then I remembered Zach saying how he once calmed a black bear that had been about to charge him by speaking quietly to it. I tried the same tactic. "There, there," I said softly. "I would rather not be gored or trampled, if you don't mind. You go your way and I will go mine."

The buffalo shook its head, as if my words were buzzing insects that annoyed it. It sniffed loudly.

I recalled something else. Zach had warned me that animals could smell fear, and that a predator might take that as a sign of easy prey. But buffalo were not predators in the true sense. They only attacked when provoked. Or so I fervently prayed.

The bull took another step.

I swore I could hear the hammering of my heart. I was near breathless with dread.

I decided to slowly back away. That would show I

posed no threat. But the instant I moved my foot, the buff rumbled and snorted and bobbed its head, its horns like twin swords.

Moving only my eyes, I glanced to the right and the left, seeking a tree I could climb. There were plenty, but none I could reach before the buffalo reached me.

Then a second shaggy form appeared. I tensed my legs to flee. But the second buffalo, a cow, gave a grunt and turned around, and the bull wheeled and followed after her. Then the whole herd, which I estimated to be about ten animals, moved off.

My relief was so profound, I grew weak in the legs. My knees nearly buckled. I smothered an impulse to laugh, afraid the sound might bring the bull back.

A hand fell on my shoulder and I almost jumped out of my skin.

"You handled that well," Zach said.

Sweat was trickling down my brow, and I mopped it with a sleeve. "You were behind me the whole time?"

Zach had my rifle as well as his, and he held mine out to me. "You forgot this."

"Would you have shot if it charged us?"

"I would do what I could."

The implication, of course, was that the bull would have killed us. "I must be more careful," I said with a pasty grin.

"You must be more careful," Zach agreed, but he was not grinning.

The next event of note occurred days later.

We came to another stream and followed it to where it forked. Zach drew rein and shifted in the saddle to inform me, "This is where I blindfold you."

"Is that really necessary?" I was mildly irritated. We had been getting along so well, and he had been so friendly, I assumed he had given up on the idea.

"You agreed," Zach reminded me.

I submitted, but I was not happy about it. He used a strip of buckskin from a parfleche.

My horse was added to the string. I know not how many miles we traveled, but it took forever. Since I did not have the reins in hand, I held to the saddle. Every dip and roll seemed worse than it would have if I could see. Why that should be I cannot say, unless it was that in being deprived of sight, my other senses were sharpened. Twice I was nearly unhorsed. Once, when a tree limb brushed my arm and I gave a start, and again when rocks were clattering from under us and my mount stumbled.

My patience came to an end, and I curtly demanded, "How much longer?"

"It is not far now."

"I hope this valley of yours is all you claim it to be." I was being petty to spite him.

"You will find out soon enough."

We had been climbing for thousands of feet. The ringing echo of the clomp of our horses suggested we were in a canyon. Then the echoes stopped, and I had the impression, by the sound of muted thuds and the rustle of leaves, that we were in a forest. "Are we there yet?" I asked.

Zach laughed.

"What do you find so amusing?"

"You remind me of my sister when she was ten."

I did not know how to take that, but it did not sound like a compliment. "You can hardly fault me," I responded. "How would you like to be led around blindfolded for mile after mile?"

"I wouldn't like it one bit."

I admired his honesty. He must have reined up because my horse came to a stop, and the next I knew, fingers were prying at the strip. We were in heavy timber. A shaft of sunlight was on my face, causing me to squint against the bright glare. Blinking, I looked about, but all I saw were trees and more trees. "Is this King Valley?"

Zach laughed again, tossed me the lead rope to my packhorse, and clucked to his own mount. "Stay behind me so you don't take an arrow."

"How is that again?"

He did not answer but goaded his bay into a trot. Eager to see his loved ones, I suspected, and I kept up with him as best I was able. To be honest, he was a far better horseman than I could ever hope to be.

Once, down on the prairie, I had been trying to sketch and ride at the same time when I dropped my sketchbook. He happened to be riding beside me at the time, and when I lifted my reins to swing around and retrieve it, he said, "Let me." And just like that, he wheeled his horse in a loop while dropping onto its side as it turned so that he hung by a forearm and an ankle. Then, as neatly as you please he snatched up my sketchbook and swung back up. All, mind you, in a fraction of the time it takes me to describe the feat. I complimented him, and he offhandedly remarked that he had learned the trick when he was seven, on his Indian pony. Seven! When I marveled at his ability, he said that it was "nothing," that if I wanted to see real riding, I should see the Comanches.

"The only problem with that," he observed matter-of-factly, "is that when you see Comanches, they are usually out to kill you."

In any event, here we were, threading through dense woodland, when up ahead I glimpsed a patch of blue that must be the lake he had mentioned now and again. I also spied something else, and it so surprised me that I drew rein in amazement. "What in the world?"

You see, Zach had told me about the three cabins I should expect. To the north of the lake was his; to the west of the lake was his father's; to the south of it stood the cabin belonging to Shakespeare McNair. But Zach had not said anything about another dwelling, one so remarkable and so out of place, that for a few seconds I was under the illusion I was in an Eastern forest and not deep in the Rockies.

Before me was a large lodge constructed of logs and intertwined limbs. In effect it was a conical mound, a type of structure I had encountered among Eastern tribes but never imagined I would come across out here. The lodge itself was unusual enough, but the entire outer surface had also been painted a vivid green.

I had barely absorbed this wonder when I beheld figures moving toward us. Indians, judging by their features and their buckskins. Their clothes, strangely enough, had been dyed the same vivid green as their lodge. The two in the lead were men, one twice as old as the other, with enough similarities of face and build to suggest they were father and son. Both were armed with bows and had arrows nocked to the strings. The youngest started to raise his, then smiled and exclaimed, "Stalking Coyote!"

I looked at Zach in puzzlement.

"My Shoshone name."

"Not that," I responded, and motioned at the lodge and the family of Indians. "You never said anything about *them*."

"Oh." Zach drew rein. "They are Nansusequa. The last of their kind. They are from east of the Mississippi. Their village and all their people were wiped out by whites who wanted their land. We are letting them live here."

He introduced me. The father was Wakumassee, the son Degamawaku. The mother was called Tihikanima, the older daughter Tenikawaku, the youngest girl was Mikikawaku. Mouthfuls, those names.

The father spoke English, although poorly. The son knew a few words, too. Zach explained that we had just arrived from Bent's Fort and he was eager to get home. He promised the Nansusequa to bring me over to visit in a day or two.

Presently, we were out of the trees and in the open air, and for the first time I saw King Valley in all its magnificent splendor. I was so dazzled, I again reined up.

The problem with language is that while words can come close to conveying our meaning, they are a poor substitute for the experiences that spawn them. In this instance, my powers of description cannot do King Valley justice. It was magnificent.

But to give you some idea: imagine an immense bowl. The bottom and sides of the bowl were green with grass and woodland. Higher up, where the timber ended, was the brown of earth and rock. Splashes of ivory crowned several of the highest peaks, and to the northwest was the white of a glacier. I asked Zach if he would take me up to see it.

"When elk sprout wings and fly," was his reply.

"What do you have against glaciers?" I figured he was joking with me.

"Only that they can kill you if you are not careful."

(I later learned that he and his wife had a harrowing experience when they went up to see it.)

The blue-green of the lake was breathtaking. The water was fed in part by runoff from the glacier. It was refreshingly cold and delicious to the taste, and so clear that I could see the bottom for up to fifty or sixty feet out.

We reined to the north and followed the shoreline. I was gazing out over the lake, noting the variety of waterfowl. There were geese and ducks galore. Scores and scores of them, some of which, unless I was grossly mistaken, were unknown to science. I couldn't wait to sketch and paint them.

Zach's cabin appeared to be remarkably well constructed. At my inquiry, he revealed that his father oversaw the work. He spoke with such pride, I gathered that the two of them were exceptionally close.

Zach rode faster. His eyes were on the cabin. He was no doubt hoping for his wife to rush out to greet him, but no one had appeared by the time we drew rein in a cloud of dust. Zach immediately swung down and ran inside, emerging moments later to inform me no one was there.

"She must be at my folks'."

We left the packhorses in the corral. Zach said we would strip them when we got back. He was so eager to see his beloved, it was humorous. But I did not laugh. Even though we were friends by now, I sensed there were certain things you did not do or say to him.

We headed for his father's cabin at the west end of the lake, riding at the water's edge. A dozen or so large white birds caught my attention. I gave a start when I recognized them as trumpeter swans. They were swimming with their heads held high in regal poise. I confess that swans are my favorites, and I made it my first order of business that as soon as I met the rest of Zach's family, I would retrieve my easel and paints and render the trumpeters on canvas.

I was watching them, entranced by their grace and beauty, when the nearby water, which was quite still since no wind was blowing, suddenly swelled upward as if thrust by some invisible force. I could not believe what I was seeing. The water rose to a height of four or five feet and then swept in a wave toward a flock of mallards. The ducks instantly took wing, quacking in alarm.

"Look there!" I cried, pointing.

Zach glanced around, but he did not show the least bit of interest in the extraordinary phenomenon.

"Don't you see it?" I excitedly asked. The strange wave was slowly subsiding. It might have been a trick of the light or my imagination, but I would have sworn a large, dark form was just below the surface.

"All the time," Zach said.

"How is that again?"

"It is the lake monster."

Chapter Ten

I refused to go on until he explained.

"You know as much as we do," Zach said. "There is something in the lake. Something big. We see its wake a lot, we see the water rise up as it just did, but we never see the thing that causes it. Not clearly enough to tell what it is."

"My word," I marveled.

"The Indians say lake creatures like this one are to be left alone, that to disturb them is bad medicine. Some tribes offer sacrifices, horses and such, so lake creatures will leave them be."

"Wait a minute," I interrupted. "Are you saying this is not the only one? That there are more of these creatures in other lakes?"

Zach nodded. "The Shoshones call them water buffalo but say they are not like buffalo at all. The Nez Perce won't go near Wallowa Lake for fear of them. Word is, the things are also in that big lake up in Flathead country."

"But what are they?" I stared out over the lake, hoping to see the swell again.

"Some tribes say they are big snakes. The Nez Perce think they're giant crayfish or lobsters."

"That's absurd," I said.

"Ask them yourself if you don't believe me. They have a legend that these things used to come out of Wallowa Lake at night from time to time to kill animals and people." Zach paused. "It gets even stranger. Although the Nez Perce swear the creatures are lobsters, they say the things have flippers."

"Flippers?"

"There is another lake off in Oregon Country where these giant lobsters are supposed to live," Zach related. "The lake is in an extinct volcano, or so I have been told."

I did not know what to make of it, but I determined to always keep one eye on the lake. "Do you believe these tales, yourself?"

Zach shrugged. "I don't dismiss them out of hand, like most whites do. "The NunumBi turned out to be true, so why not lake monsters?"

I was developing the habit of repeating what he said. "NunumBi?" But he rode on without responding.

It came to me that perhaps I should include a section on Indian legends in my journal. Strictly speaking, they are not the province of a naturalist, but they would be of interest to those who studied folklore and the like.

I was so deep in thought that I fell farther behind than I intended. At a shout from Zach I glanced up. He was fifty yards away, jabbing a finger at me.

"Look out! It's heading your way!"

I turned toward the lake, thinking he referred to the lake creature, but the surface was tranquil and undisturbed. Then I heard a mewing sound, and turning toward where a finger of forest poked at the shore, I saw a bear cub waddling toward me. A black bear cub, so cute and adorable I grinned in delight. Apparently, it was making for the lake to drink.

"Get out of there!" Zach hollered.

The cub had its head low to the ground and was mewing and grunting as bears often do. It did not realize I was there until I reined my mount to one side. Instantly, it stopped, rose onto its hind legs, and let out with the most awful cry. Almost immediately the undergrowth crackled and snapped, and out of the woods flew four hundred pounds of motherly fury.

Jabbing my heels, I galloped toward Zach. I reasoned that when the mother bear saw me move away from her cub, she would no longer consider me a threat.

"Ride, Robert, ride!"

The mother bear had not slowed. In fact, she was angling to intercept me, and moving with amazing speed. Over short distances bears can outrun horses, and she was rapidly overtaking mine.

"Shoot her!" Zach shouted. He had reined around and was racing to my aid.

I refused to do any such thing. She was only protecting her young. I still thought I could escape, and goaded my horse to go faster. My effort was too little, too late.

Hurtling headlong, the mother bear slammed into my mount broadside. The impact bowled us over, and my horse shrieked in terror. I pushed free of the saddle to avoid being crushed. I was successful, but instead of landing on my side and rolling away, as I intended, I came down in the lake. The water wasn't deep, no more than knee high, but I got it in my eyes and my nose and came up blinking and sputtering. For a few seconds everything was a blur. Then my vision cleared, and I saw that my horse had scrambled upright and was fleeing.

The mother bear let it go.

She was more interested in me.

Not six feet separated us. Her hackles were up and her teeth were bared. Rage incarnate, she intended to rip me limb from limb.

Zach was bellowing for me to shoot her.

I still had my rifle, but it had gone under the water. It would probably misfire. I had a pistol, but that, too, had gotten wet. Even if I could use them, though, I wouldn't. As I have already stressed, I refrain from killing when at all possible.

My noble purpose notwithstanding, she was in a bestial frenzy, and in another instant would charge.

Then hooves pounded, and Zach went flying by. He let out a whoop, perhaps to draw the mother bear's attention, and slid onto the side of his horse, as he had done that day he snatched up my sketchbook. Only this time it was the cub he snatched. Exhibiting uncanny skill, he grabbed hold of the scruff of its neck, yanked it off the ground and swung back up.

The cub squalled in terror.

At that, the mother bear whirled. In a heartbeat she was off after Zach. He had reined toward the forest, and when he was almost there, he again swung onto the side of his horse and dropped the cub gently to the ground. It rolled and came up unscathed. Zach did not stop; he rode in a half circle that would bring him back to me.

As for the mother bear, she reached her offspring and without seeming to break stride, caught the cub up in her mouth. In the bat of an eye they were in among the trees. The racket raised by her flight soon faded.

I shuffled out of the lake and let out a breath I had not realized I was holding.

Zach came to a stop and looked down at me. "What got into you? You didn't even try to kill her."

"You didn't either, I noticed," I responded.

"It is hard to aim from horseback," Zach said. "I didn't want to risk wounding her and making her madder."

I grinned. "Pretend all you want, but I know the truth about you now."

"Which truth would that be?"

"You are a fraud, Zachary King. You have a reputation for being a savage killer when you are no such thing. You are as tenderhearted as I or the next person."

Voices ended our banter. People were running toward us, and several of them were calling out Zach's name. He dismounted.

I had been told enough about them that I knew who they were before I was introduced.

Louisa King, Zach's wife, was a petite bundle of energy in buckskins. Short sandy hair lent her a boyish aspect. Her eyes were the same bright blue as the lake. Squealing in delight, she threw herself at her husband and wrapped her slender arms tight. "I've missed you!"

Next to arrive was a tall, broad-shouldered man whose green eyes, high cheekbones and strong jaw were mirror images of Zach's. Or should I say it was the other way around? For this was Zach's sire, Nate King, a mountain man ranked with the likes of Kit Carson and Jim Bridger, according to Ceran St. Vrain. The father, too, wore buckskins, and he, like Zach, was a walking armory.

The woman at Nate's side had to be his Shoshone wife, Winona. She was quite lovely. I read in her an uncommon alertness and intelligence. Zach had said she possessed a tender temperament, and I could read that, as well, in the loving gaze she bestowed on him. She wore a beautiful doeskin dress decorated with blue beads.

A girl of sixteen or so proved to be Zach's sister, Evelyn King. Where Zach had more of his mother in him, she had more of her father. Not that she was unattractive. Far from it. She was adorable. She also wore a dress, but a dress such as women on the streets of St. Louis or New Orleans would wear. She was the only one of the Kings who did not wear moccasins. Her footwear? Ordinary shoes.

An older couple were the last to arrive. The man's hair and beard were as white as pristine snow. He had to be in his seventies or eighties, yet his vitality was that of someone half his age. His craggy face glowed with warmth and friendliness, and I took an immediate liking to him. He could be none other than Shakespeare McNair.

McNair's Flathead wife was known as Blue Water Woman. She was quiet, almost shy. Her hair had a few gray streaks, but otherwise she did not look her age. Her dress was also adorned with beads, but her beads were red and yellow, not blue. She was quite exquisite, more so to me than the other women. Why that should be, who can say?

These, then, were the Kings and their dearest friends. They greeted me cordially enough.

Nate King's hand was twice the size of mine. He shook firmly while scrutinizing me from head to toe. "So you are a naturalist?"

"I hope my visit will not be an imposition."

"We don't get many visitors," Nate said. He did not add "I like it that way," but that is the feeling he gave me. Instead he said, "My son vouches for you. You are welcome to stay as long as you want."

"Thank you."

Winona and Evelyn were models of decorum. Then it was Shakespeare McNair's turn. He worked my arm as if it were a pump lever and gave a mock bow.

"'Here, Winchester, I offer thee my hand,'" he quoted. "'I bid thee greetings.'"

"I am pleased to make your acquaintance, sir," I said. "Your notoriety precedes you."

"All mimicry, I am afraid," Shakespeare said. "'Oh, for a Muse of fire that would ascend the brightest heaven of invention.'"

"Is that from *King John*?" I asked.

"*Henry the Fifth*," Shakespeare corrected. "You are familiar with the Bard, then?"

"A few of his works," I admitted. "But nowhere near the degree you are."

"A little is better than none." Shakespeare nodded at Nate King. "For years I have been trying to get Horatio there to appreciate the Bard as much as I do, but he would rather read the likes of Cooper, Irving and Scott. Which shows there is no taste like no taste."

Nate chuckled. "I will have you know James Fenimore Cooper's works are as good as your namesake's any day."

Shakespeare pressed a hand to his chest and took a step back as if in shock. "Did my ears hear aright? 'Methink's thou art a general offense and every man should beat thee.'"

I could not help but laugh.

"Pay him no mind," Nate said to me. "He prattles on like this constantly. I can lend you bits of cotton to stick in your ears if need be."

McNair sputtered, then exclaimed dramatically,

"'There can be no kernel in this light nut! The soul of this man is in his clothes.'"

"Honestly, now," Nate said. "Do you want Mr. Parker to think you are not in your right mind?"

"I find the ass in compound with the major part of your syllables," Shakespeare jousted.

Again I laughed. "'A hit,'" I quoted from *Hamlet*. "'A very palpable hit.'"

To my consternation, McNair seized me by the shoulders and kissed me roughly on the cheek. "Did you hear him, Horatio? He knows! He *knows*! I believe I am in love."

"Please, sir," I said, disentangling myself. "Constrain yourself. You are spoken for, in case you have forgotten."

Nate King cackled and clapped McNair on the back. "That is what you get for not using English like the rest of us."

"English!" Shakespeare roared. "Are you a simpleton? Is the Bard from Norway, then?"

"I seem to recollect he scribbled most of his lines in a place called Avon," Nate said.

"Scribbled?"

I would swear McNair was fit to burst a vein.

That was when Blue Water Woman said quietly, "Enough, husband."

Shakespeare turned to her, his mock outrage evaporating in a twinkling. "As you wish, love of my life."

"Robert Parker will think your head is in a whirl," Blue Water Woman said. "Behave yourself for a while so he can see you are sane."

Nate snickered.

"From your heart to mine," Shakespeare said to her quite tenderly. Then he looked at me, grinned, and

winked. "But mark you, hoss. This truce is temporary."
To Nate he said, "As for you, you ox, you are lucky I
don't dunk you in the lake."

"Do that," I said, "and the monster might get him."

"Heard about that thing, have you?" Shakespeare
said, and faced the water.

"I saw it," I explained. "Or, rather, the swell it
caused."

"Ah. I have seen that swell more times than I can
count," Shakespeare said. "It baffles me, and I do not
like being baffled. Before the summer is done, I mean
to find out what causes it."

"How?"

McNair was about to answer when he unexpectedly stiffened and pointed at the valley rim to the
east. "Look there!" he cried.

I glanced over my shoulder and spotted a flash of
light, as of sunlight off metal. All the others were staring, and their faces were grim. "What's wrong?" I
asked.

It was Nate King who answered. "We have visitors,
and visitors nearly always spell trouble."

Chapter Eleven

The effect of that flash of light was remarkable.

Nate and Shakespeare rushed off to get their horses. Winona and Blue Water Woman hustled the younger women toward Nate's cabin. I was left with Zach, who was intently watching the rim.

"Damn me for a fool."

"Why?"

"I was careless," Zach said. "We were followed all the way here." He pointed. "Look! There it is again."

Indeed, the flash was repeated in the same spot as before, only this time it persisted for several seconds before blinking out.

"What do you make of it?" I inquired.

"Whoever is up there is using a spyglass," Zach said. "Which means they are up to no good." He indulged in a rare burst of lurid swearing.

"You are guessing."

"It's a good guess," Zach replied. "If they were friendly, why didn't they show themselves to us on the way here?"

"They?"

"No white man would come this far into the mountains alone."

I was thinking of his trick with the talus and the stream we had ridden in for so many miles. I reminded him of them.

"It wouldn't shake a good tracker off our scent."

"What will you do if you are right and you catch them?"

"It depends."

"On what?"

"On who they are and why they are here," Zach said.

"What if they refused to tell you?"

His smile was chilling. "Whether they want to or not, they will."

Presently, his father and McNair came galloping from the cabin. I swung on my horse, which Zach had recovered, and Zach and I fell in behind them as they swept by. I must confess, I thought they were far more agitated than the occasion warranted.

That ride was something. We fairly flew around the lake. When we reached the green lodge of the Nansusequa, we stopped long enough for Nate King to inform them of what was going on. "Keep a close watch," he said to Wakumassee. "We'll let you know what we find."

Then we were off again. We climbed through the heavy timber until we neared a wide cleft that turned out to be the mouth of a canyon. It was here Nate drew rein and alighted. Shakespeare was quick to join him. Bent at the waist, they scoured the ground. After a while they straightened and looked at one another, and I could tell they were puzzled.

"Deucedly strange, Horatio," Shakespeare said.

"Or clever," Nate responded.

Zach stirred. "There aren't any tracks, Pa?"

"The most recent are yours and Mr. Parker's and your packhorses," Nate said.

"There are a few spots where the grass has been bent since but no clear prints," Shakespeares said. "Odds are they cut up a blanket and tied the pieces over their horses' hooves."

Nate stepped to his mount, opened a parfleche, and took out a shiny brass tube. A flick of his wrist, and the tube telescoped into a spyglass. He spent several minutes surveying the woods and the valley floor. Finally he scowled and lowered it. "No sign of anyone."

"They have to be somewhere," Zach said.

"'Indeed, indeed, sirs, but this troubles me,'" Shakespeare quoted.

I felt I must contribute, and so, motivated by my doubts, I remarked, "Perhaps we are overreacting."

Nate King gave me a kindly smile. "Our families are here. Our loved ones. Our friends. Threats to their lives must be met swiftly."

"But we don't even know there *is* a threat," I said.

Shakespeare wagged a finger at me. "Would you have us be like Caesar and ignore the portents? Constant vigilance is the price we must pay if we would go on living where we will."

Part of me agreed, but another part felt a tad silly. "What now?"

"We split up," Nate King said. "Shakespeare and I will swing to the south. Zach, you and Mr. Parker try the north. Work your way down and stay alert for sign. Fire two shots in the air if you find anything."

I was in no mood for this. I was tired and hungry and had relished the idea of spending the rest of the day resting. But they were my hosts, I their guest, and it would be remiss of me not to help them. Still, since I cannot track, there was little I could do other than follow after Zach and watch for evidence of anything out of the ordinary.

We roved back and forth for over an hour, gradually descending until we were once again at the lake shore. Once there, Zach drew rein in disgust.

"Nothing."

"Maybe we are mistaken," I suggested. By "we" I meant "them," but I was being tactful.

At that moment his father and McNair emerged from the woods to the south of the lake. Nate spotted us and waved, and they came around to meet us at Nate's cabin. By the look on his face, it was plain they had not found the sign they were looking for.

"Not so much as a trace," Nate confirmed.

"All we can do is wait," Shakespeare said, and once again reached into his bottomless bag of quotes. "'It is the rankest compound of villainous smell that ever offended nostril.'"

"If you are saying it stinks, I agree," Zach said.

I sought to be the voice of reason. "It could be they will prove to be friendly."

"'One may smile and smile, and be a villain,'" Shakespeare quoted.

Nate cleared his throat. "This is what we will do. I will go warn Waku and his family to stay on their guard. The rest of you wait here. We will have supper together, and later decide our course of action for tomorrow."

As he trotted off, I turned to McNair. "Permit me to compliment you on your knowledge of the Bard."

Shakespeare reached back and patted a parfleche. "I never go anywhere without my copy of his works. Every spare minute, I spend reading him."

"Might I ask why? I mean, why him as opposed to some other writer?"

"There are no others. They are all imitators. Old William S was the genuine article."

"It is the last thing I would expect," I said.

"Why? Because trappers and mountain men are supposed to be brainless clods who can't read or write?" McNair clucked in disapproval. "Let me tell you something. Back in the days when beaver was in demand, the trappers would hole up for the winter. And do you know what they spent their days doing? Every hour from dawn until dusk, and often after by candlelight? They read. They collected every book they could get their hands on and devoured them from beginning to end. The Bible was one, of course. Sir Walter Scott's works. Washington Irving. Jane Austen. The poets, Byron and Shelley and Keats. A favorite of most was that novel by Shelley's wife, the one about the creature made of dead parts." He paused. "We read, and we talked about what we had read, then we read some more. The Rocky Mountain College, we called it, and there was never a college anywhere from which men learned more."

"I had no idea," I said.

"Most don't. A lot of folks back east think all frontiersmen are filthy, uneducated louts. And some are. But as many or more can hold their own in any talk about literature and religion, and are cleanly in their habits, as well."

I smiled. "You make a staunch defender."

He returned my smile. "I like you, hoss. You don't put on as many airs as some do. You are too soft, but if you stay out here long enough, the wilderness will cure you of that."

"Soft?" I said.

"You think the world is a friendly place and it's not."

"How can you say that when you have known me such a short while?" I asked.

"You thought we were wasting our time hunting for whoever is in our valley. I could see it on your face."

"Evidently you read people like you read books," I said. "And you are right. I confess that I do not see an enemy or a beast behind every tree."

"It might be better for you if you did," Shakespeare advised. "Better to be wary than dead."

Food for thought, but I could not change my ways at the snap of a finger.

The women came out and listened to McNair's recital of our search. Winona announced that we would eat in a couple of hours, and she kindly asked me if I wanted to rest until then.

I was tired but also fired with enthusiasm. Already I had espied a few woodland birds and several waterfowl unknown to me, and I was eager to capture them on paper. Accordingly, I grabbed my sketchbook and headed around the lake on foot, seeking a particular duck. I had not gone far when I heard footfalls behind me and was taken aback to discover Blue Water Woman hurrying to catch up. She was armed with a rifle and a brace of pistols.

"What is this?" I asked.

"We don't want you wandering off alone, Robert Parker," she responded in that soft voice of hers. "Since Winona is busy cooking and Evelyn is helping her, and Zach just got back and Lou wants to spend time with him, I volunteered."

I was surprised her husband had not come, and said so.

"He wanted to, but I have not been out much today and can use the exercise." Blue Water Woman absently ran a hand through her long hair. Her smooth complexion belied the streaks of gray.

"This is kind of you, but unecessary." I patted my pistol. "I can look after myself."

"No, you can't."

"I beg your pardon?"

"You are an innocent, was how Zach put it. My husband agrees. You are used to the tame forests of the East."

I was mildly miffed. Here I was, a grown man, being treated as if I were five years old. But rather than hurt her feelings, I said, "Come along, then. And may I say how impressed I am by your English."

"Living with that white-haired lunatic has been an education," Blue Water Woman said with a grin. "But when it comes to learning new tongues, I cannot hold a candle to Winona. She is a born linguist."

"I had imagined you would communicate with your husband through sign language, or in your own language."

"We do that, too. I speak four tongues, not counting my own."

"My word."

"Winona speaks twice as many and has a smattering of others. Nate says her English is better than his."

"I look forward to talking to her." I turned to the lake and scanned it for the ducks I was interested in sketching. Their plumage was brown with green on the wings and around the eyes. But I did not spot any.

"My husband tells me you are something called a naturalist," Blue Water Woman said. "That your work is to study animals, how they look and how they live."

"I have loved animals all my life. Even as a small child I would spend hours a day studying the bugs and birds in our yard."

"It is important, this work you do?"

"I think it is. The more we know about the world around us, about the creatures we share it with, the better we can get along with those creatures."

"Get along how?"

"I have this dream," I said, and stopped. I had been laughed at so many times that I was loathe to be ridiculed again.

"I am listening."

"You will think it silly."

Blue Water Woman smiled. "Naturalists can predict what people will think? How remarkable."

I stopped and faced her. She seemed to be sincere so I decided to air my innermost self. "Do you remember when beaver fur was all the fashion for whites? And white men overran these mountains, trapping every stream and river?"

"Of course," Blue Water Woman said. "My husband trapped for a while. So did Nate King."

"And what happened?" I answered my question before she could. "I will tell you. The beaver were almost wiped out."

"For a while there were hardly any, yes. But in recent years we see more and more of them."

"The same thing has happened to a lot of animals east of the Mississippi. In some states wolves and cougars have been exterminated. In others, game which was once abundant is now scarce. Most people don't seem to care, but I do. I think we should respect the right of all creatures to walk this earth with us, and not wipe them out because we are afraid of them or because they are a nuisance."

"My people believe we should live in harmony with all things, too," Blue Water Woman said quietly.

"My own kind care only about themselves. They

take what they want, and the consequences be hanged. If animals like beaver are wiped out, no one cares. They don't seem to realize that once an animal is gone, it is gone forever. I say that is wrong. And I hope, by my studies, to show how we can get along with the animals that share our world so that we don't have to wipe out any more of them."

Blue Water Woman studied me, then placed a hand on my shoulder and gently squeezed. "I like you, Robert Parker. You are a good man. You have my friendship for as long as you want it."

I thought my ears were on fire. "Thank you."

She started to say something, glanced past me at the water, and her eyes widened.

I turned.

The thing in the lake had created another swell. Even as we watched, a long form briefly appeared, then dived.

Blue Water Woman smiled. "It is a delight to see."

"Yes, it is," I said. But I was looking at her.

Chapter Twelve

The next week was a joy.

I spent every waking minute either sketching or painting or writing in my journal. Wildlife was everywhere, and I caught on canvas two new waterfowl, three songbirds, and a mouse never before recorded. The plant life was equally fertile, with varieties not found east of the Mississippi.

My explorations took me all over the valley floor and adjacent slopes. My hosts let me do as I pleased, and I must say, their hospitality was beyond reproach. My only nitpick was that they would not let me go anywhere alone. They continued to treat me as if I could not lace up my boots without help. I resented it, but my resentment waned as I came to relish the company of the person who served as my nursemaid.

That person was Blue Water Woman.

I hardly saw Zach. He had been away from his wife for so long that they sequestered themselves in their cabin and rarely came out. Winona hinted that they were hoping to start a family, so I could guess what they were up to.

Nate spent a lot of time prowling the valley in search of the intruders he felt certain were hiding somewhere.

Shakespeare McNair was busy building a raft, of all things. He had determined to get to the bottom of the mystery of the thing in the lake, and he intended, once the raft was done, to try and catch it.

I saw nothing of the Indians in the green lodge. Well, except for the young man, Dega, who came regularly to go on long strolls with Evelyn King. Unless I was mistaken, a romance was blooming.

Winona had too many chores to do about the cabin and in her garden. She accompanied me a few times, but the rest of the time it was Blue Water Woman, who had taken a keen interest in my work and was fascinated by my lifelike portraits and drawings. Although she was twice my age, if not more, and from a different culture, we shared an affinity of spirit. She was very much interested in the natural world and the creatures in it. But then, many Indians are, simply because they must relate to it each and every day in a manner many whites cannot conceive.

Civilization serves to separate whites from the natural order. Town and city dwellers do not need to kill their food, or skin game for hides to make their clothes. They get all they need by buying it. An artificial order is in place, a system, I am afraid, that separates us from the world in which we live.

Farmers grow and make their own food, but even many of them no longer make their clothes when apparel may so readily be purchased. They are close to the earth, but not as close as the Indians, who are so much a part of it that they depend on the creatures about them for their very existence.

I admit it. I admire the red man. They have learned to adapt to nature rather than control it. They share the world with everything around them; they do not conquer for the sake of conquering. Perhaps it is silly

GET
4 FREE BOOKS!

You can have the best Westerns delivered to your door for less than what you'd pay in a bookstore or online. Sign up for one of our book clubs today, and we'll send you **4 FREE* BOOKS**, worth $23.96, just for trying it out...**with no obligation to buy, ever!**

Authors include classic writers such as
LOUIS L'AMOUR, MAX BRAND, ZANE GREY
and more; PLUS new authors such as
COTTON SMITH, TIM CHAMPLIN, JOHNNY D. BOGGS
and others.

As a book club member you also receive the following special benefits:

- **30% OFF** all orders through our website & telecenter!
- **Exclusive access** to special discounts!
- **Convenient** home delivery **and 10 days to return any books you don't want to keep.**

There is no minimum number of books to buy,
and you may cancel membership at any time.
See back to sign up!

*Please include $2.00 for shipping and handling.

YES! ☐

Sign me up for the Leisure Western Book Club
and send my FOUR FREE BOOKS! If I choose to stay
in the club, I will pay only $14.00* each month,
a savings of $9.96!

NAME: _____

ADDRESS: _____

_____

TELEPHONE: _____

E-MAIL: _____

☐ I WANT TO PAY BY CREDIT CARD.

☐ VISA   ☐ MasterCard   ☐ DISCOVER

ACCOUNT #: _____

EXPIRATION DATE: _____

SIGNATURE: _____

Send this card along with $2.00 shipping & handling to:

**Leisure Western Book Club
1 Mechanic Street
Norwalk, CT 06850-3431**

Or fax (must include credit card information!) to: 610.995.9274.
You can also sign up online at www.dorchesterpub.com.

*Plus $2.00 for shipping. Offer open to residents of the U.S. and Canada only.
Canadian residents please call 1.800.481.9191 for pricing information.
If under 18, a parent or guardian must sign. Terms, prices and conditions subject to change. Subscription subject
to acceptance. Dorchester Publishing reserves the right to reject any order or cancel any subscription.

of me but I wish my own kind could learn from the Indians and come to regard all living things with the respect I feel all creatures deserve.

Blue Water Woman shared my belief. We talked about it many times. That, and many other subjects. She was remarkably well versed in white ways and had learned a lot about white history from her husband.

On the eighth morning after my arrival in King Valley, I proposed to ride up to the glacier. Zach had mentioned a small bird found in its vicinity and nowhere else. My curiosity was piqued. Accordingly, I had my packhorse and my mount ready to depart at first light. No sooner did I climb on and take the lead rope in hand than around the corner of Nate's cabin came Blue Water Woman on a fine mare.

"I told you that you need not come," I said by way of greeting. "I have already imposed on your gracious nature enough."

"Good morning, Robert Parker," she said. "I have nothing better to do, and I like your company."

"Very well. But there is a chance I will not make it back by nightfall. What will your husband say, you alone with another man?"

"If you imply he would be jealous, you are mistaken," Blue Water Woman replied. "He knows I would kill any man who laid a hand on me. And I know you would never do that, gentleman that you are."

"Of course I wouldn't," I said, my throat constricted. I clucked to my horse and we were off.

A stiff breeze out of the northwest caressed my skin. Out on the lake the geese and ducks were huddled close together, while in the forest the songbirds were filling the air with their first warbles of the new day.

It felt glorious to be alive. I savored the pulse of life

in all its myriad variety—moments like these were the moments I lived for.

Blue Water Woman let me lead where I would. She did comment that using a game trail would be easier on the horses, but I was having too much fun exploring. Again and again a plant or an animal would spark my interest and I would rein to one side or the other. Now and then I glimpsed the white of the glacier far above, ensuring I did not drift too far afield.

Most of the morning had gone by when we entered a belt of firs. Arrayed in tall phalanx, they did not permit the sunlight to reach the forest floor. Shadowy gloom shrouded us.

Suddenly wings fluttered to my left, and I glanced up to see a bird in flight. We had spooked it. I saw it only for an instant, but I would swear it was a small owl.

My pulse quickened. The owls of the Rockies were not well documented, and it could be that the one I had seen was not a juvenile of a known species but a new species altogether. Accordingly, I slapped my legs against my horse and took off after it.

The firs were so closely spaced that I was constantly reining one way or the other to avoid them. I glimpsed the owl again and could not identify it.

We must have gone a hundred yards or more when the firs abruptly ended near the bank of a swift-flowing stream. Disappointed, I came to a stop. "I suppose this is as good a spot as any to rest the horses."

"Did you want to paint that owl you were chasing?" Blue Water Woman asked.

"Do you know what kind it was? I mean, the name whites call it?"

Her brow knit, and she shook her head. "So far as I know, Robert Parker, it does not have a white name."

"Then it must be a new species!" I declared, thrilled at the prospect of being its discoverer. "After we rest we must look for it or another of its kind."

"They usually only come out at night," Blue Water Woman said. "To see one during the day is rare."

"I must try." I dismounted and led my mount and packhorse to the stream. She followed suit with her animal. I doubt she was aware of it, but she possessed a natural grace I greatly admired. That, and her perpetual calm. I never saw Blue Water Woman upset or flustered.

One day at the lake she had slipped on a rock and fell, banging her knee. She did not throw a fit of temper, as I would have done. Instead, she calmly got back up and smoothed her buckskin dress.

"Didn't that hurt?" I asked.

"Yes," she answered. She tested her leg, limping with each step. "But the pain will soon go away."

"You are always so composed, so in control of yourself," I mentioned. "Doesn't anything fluster you?"

"My husband, when he leaves his dirty clothes lying around, or when he butchers an animal outside our door and does not bury the remains, or when he goes off somewhere and does not tell me where he is going and then he is gone for hours on end—" Blue Water Woman stopped, and self-consciously grinned. "You men have a knack for flustering us women."

I chuckled. "For all that, you love him very much, don't you?"

She gazed down the mountain at the cabins along the lake and a longing came into her lovely eyes. At that instant I envied Shakespeare McNair as I never envied anyone. "I love my husband with all I am. He is everything to me. Were he to die, I would slit my wrists so I could follow after him."

"You shouldn't talk like that," I chided.

"I speak my heart, Robert Parker. For all his silliness, Shakespeare is everything to me. My breath, my life. I heard someone say once that it is possible to love too much, but I say that too much is never enough."

"McNair is a lucky fellow. I would give anything to be in his boots." I quickly added, "And have a woman who cares for me as deeply as you care for him."

"If you look for a wife as devotedly as you look for birds, you will find her," Blue Water Woman said.

I often wondered about that. I am a man; I have certain urges. But I have never given any thought to a family and a home. My relationships have all been dalliances of the flesh more than anything. How, then, am I to find a woman willing to spend the rest of her days with me? It would help if I stopped traipsing all over creation, but I am not about to quit anytime soon. Heaven help me, I would rather devote myself to science than to a wife.

As if she were able to read my thoughts, Blue Water Woman said, "Give yourself time, Robert Parker. You are fairly young yet. When that special woman comes along, you will know."

I changed the subject. "Tell me, fair lady. Can you write?"

"Yes, my husband taught me. I do not do it as well as Winona, but it is legible. Why do you ask?"

"It would benefit me immensely if you could make a list of all the animals you know which do not have a white name and where to find them."

"There is a purpose to this?"

"Odds are, if they do not have a white name, they have not been discovered. Those are exactly the animals I came west to find. A list would save me a lot of time and effort."

"It will take a while, but for you I will do it."

Again my ears burned. "You can start now if you want." I brought her a pad and bid her sit on a log. My head was swimming with all the new species I might find. I would be famous. My discoveries would be on the front page of every newspaper. I would be hailed as the leading naturalist of my day and might secure a prestigious position at a university. I did not become a naturalist for fame and fortune, but neither was I averse to recognition and a comfortable income.

I walked to the stream and knelt. Cupping my hands in the cold water, I splashed my face and neck. It brought me out of myself, out of my fancies and to the here and now.

"Do you want every animal I can think of?" Blue Water Woman asked. "Snakes and bugs as well?"

"Everything without a white name, yes," I reiterated. "No matter what kind, no matter how big or how small."

"It will be a long list."

"Good!" The more new species I discovered, the better. I went to the packhorse and got out my journal, figuring I might as well catch up on my entries. I became so absorbed in my observations and descriptions that when a shadow fell across me, I gave a start.

It was Blue Water Woman. "I am finished." She held out the paper to me. "If I have not written enough I can add more."

She had done a marvelous job. First, she had listed birds, then mammals, then reptiles, then insects. She even put down a short list of fish. To give but one example, her first bird was *"A small brown hawk that hunts above the timberline. It has a yellow beak and big eyes."* She had numbered them. I ran my finger down the list to the last and exclaimed, "Thirty-nine? That many?"

"It could be that whites know of some of them, but I do not know the white name because when my husband and I talked about them, we talked in my own tongue."

"McNair speaks Flathead?" I stupidly asked.

"Fluently. With a memory as good as his, he learns new tongues easily. Not as easily as Winona, but close."

"You keep bringing her up," I said.

"She is my best friend. I am in awe of how quickly she learns things. What would take me six months, she learns in a week."

"You exaggerate, surely." I scanned her list again, and something gave me pause. "Wait a minute. What is this? You wrote here, 'A giant bird that carries off buffalo and sometimes people.'"

"Yes. My people call them thunderbirds. It has been many winters since they were last seen, but in my grandfather's time my people lived in great fear of them."

"So you have never seen one yourself? This is more of a legend?"

"You said everything, big or small," Blue Water Woman reminded me. "I did not write about the giants or the little men, though, since they are people like you and me."

"The what?"

"Long ago, when my people, the Salish, first came to the country where they now live, they fought with giants who lived in caves and wore bearskins. From time to time one would sneak into a Salish village at night and steal a woman."

"Legends," I stressed.

Blue Water Woman did not seem to hear me. "The

little people had dark skins. They lived in the thickest woods where it was hard for men to travel, and they would signal one another by beating on a tree with a stick. The bow was the weapon they liked best. They made pictures on rocks, but no one could read what the pictures said."

"Honestly, now," I interrupted. These accounts bordered on fairy tales. "And where are the giants and the dwarfs now?"

"The giants were killed off long ago. They were a terror and had to be stopped. The dwarfs did not hurt anyone, so the Salish left them alone. My grandfather saw one when he was a boy."

I was about to say how preposterous all of this was when a jay took wing squawking on the other side of the stream, and a few moments later, a handful of sparrows, twittering noisily, did the same.

Blue Water Woman raised her rifle. "On your feet, Robert Parker. We are not alone."

Chapter Thirteen

Anything could have spooked the birds, and I said so.

"We must hide, quickly," Blue Water Woman insisted. She did not wait for me to reply but turned and hastened to the horses.

I was slow to rise. In my estimation her alarm was uncalled for. Yet another example of the senseless dread displayed by the McNairs and the Kings. They acted as if everything and everyone were out to get them. For grown adults to behave so childishly was silly.

"Hurry," Blue Water Woman urged.

"We have seen no sign of anyone else all day," I mentioned. "What makes you think we are in danger?"

"Please, Robert Parker."

"That is another thing," I said. "Why do you call me by my full name? Robert will do. Or even Bob, if you like."

"I like how your name sounds." Blue Water Woman turned, leading her horse, but she only took a couple of steps. Then she abruptly stopped and started to raise her rifle to her shoulder.

"I wouldn't, were I you, squaw. Not unless you want me to shoot you smack between the eyes."

It was Jess Hook. He had come up out of the woods, his rifle trained on her. I suppose I should not have been surprised, but I was. I started to jerk my own rifle when a gruff voice behind me froze me in place.

Jordy Hook had stepped from the trees across the stream. He, too, had his rifle to his shoulder, only his was aimed at me. "Set that long gun down, painter man, or I'll drop you where you stand."

"What's the meaning of this?" I demanded while complying.

Cutter appeared, leading their horses. "Listen to him, will you?" he said to Jordy. "Dumb as a stump. The airs he puts on, you'd think he had a brain between his ears."

"Now see here," I said angrily.

Jordy and Cutter forded the stream. Their wet moccasins squished as they came up the bank. Their expressions were as cold as ice.

It did not bode well. But I refused to show fear. Instead, I faced Jess Hook and said, "No one has answered me. What is this about? What do you hope to prove?"

"Prove?" Jess said, and snorted. "Mister, you beat all. I will make everything clear, but first you and your friend will shuck your pistols and knives. Nice and slow if you know what's good for you."

I obeyed promptly. Blue Water Woman did so with reluctance, earning a bark of impatience from Jordy.

Only after she had laid down her weapons did Jess Hook lower his rifle to his waist, although he continued to point it at her. "Well now. That's better. Suppose you get a fire going, Indian. Not a big one, mind, and don't use green wood to make a lot of smoke for your friends in the valley to see. I am wise to tricks like that."

Without saying a word, Blue Water Woman moved toward the trees. The instant she did, Cutter was at her side, his hand on one of his knives. He leered at her, but she ignored him.

"Don't you touch her," Jess Hook said.

Cutter glanced sharply at him. "Who are you to say yes or no? We're partners, ain't we?"

"We need her in one piece, or have you forgotten why we've gone to all this trouble?" was Jess Hook's rejoinder.

Frowning, Cutter swore, then said, "I still think we should have grabbed the girl and not these two. Nate King is more likely to give in if it's the fruit of his loins."

"She hasn't given us the chance, has she? Or would you rather wait around a month or two in the hope she waltzes into our arms?"

"I was only saying," Cutter said. Then the forest closed around him and Blue Water Woman.

I looked at Jordy Hook, who snickered.

"You've stepped in it now, painter man. You should've stayed back East where the sheep don't have to worry about wolves."

Jess Hook stepped to the log Blue Water Woman had been sitting on and beckoned to me. "Get over here and plant yourself, mister. You and me need to have words."

I did not like having rifles pointed at me, nor the implied threats of violence. "You can't treat us like this," I protested. "It isn't right."

"What the hell does that have to do with anything?" Jess snapped as I sat on the log.

"Have you no scruples?" I asked.

Jess glanced at Jordy and both brothers laughed. Then Jess placed a foot on the end of the log and leaned an elbow on his leg.

"Mister, I'll let you in on a secret. All that stuff about right and wrong, scruples as you call them, is a bunch of hogwash. It is how those who have the money and make the laws keep the rest of us in line. But you know what?" Jess leaned toward me. "It's just words. They don't mean anything. There is no right or wrong. There are no scruples. We can do as we want, and the rest of the world be damned."

"There are higher laws than man's," I said stiffly.

"Meaning the Bible?" Again the brothers swapped amused glances. "When I was little I believed in it. My folks sent me to Sunday school, and my pa read from it every evening when we set down to supper. I heard how God punishes those who do evil and rewards those who do right. But you know what?"

I rose to the bait. "What?"

"It just ain't so. The first time I killed I man, I looked up at the sky expecting a thunderbolt to come down out of the blue and fry me to a cinder. But nothing happened. The same with the second time and the third. I've killed and robbed a heap of people, and the Almighty has never lifted a finger to stop me."

"There is no God," Jordy Hook declared. "No devil, neither. No heaven and no hell."

"Fairy tales," Jess said. "We're born and we live a spell and we die. That's it."

Jordy nodded. "So we might as well help ourselves to whatever strikes our fancy along the way."

Deeply troubled, I responded with, "You're wrong, both of you. There is more to life than nothingness. Laws are not passed merely to control people, but so that everyone is treated fairly and with justice. As for the Bible, even if you deny it is divinely inspired, there is no denying the wisdom it contains."

"And the Almighty?" Jess mocked me. "I suppose you think there is a God up there somewhere who gives a hoot about us?"

"I am a man of science, not religion," I replied. "I do not claim to have all the answers. But when I see the beauty of a rose, or a butterfly's wing, and think of life in all its many forms and guises and how everything relates one to the other, yes, I believe there is *something* out there that is greater than us, and above us and in us and in all things. Call it God. Call it whatever you like. But it is there."

"It can't be much of anything if it lets us kill and get away with it," Jess Hook said.

"I told you I don't have all the answers," I said. "But this I do know: whether by God's hand or man's, you will be served your comeuppance for your foul deeds."

The Hook brothers erupted into near hysterics. Jordy bent over and slapped his leg. I failed to appreciate the comedy and told them so.

"You are a caution, painter man," Jordy said between guffaws. "We've met a lot of folks like you. Simpletons who reckon the world is like that rose you mentioned, when it's really a patch of thorns."

Jess Hook nodded. "Even if you're right, God's laws don't matter. Man's laws don't matter. The only law that does is this." He patted his rifle. "Take what we want, when we want."

When you hear someone talk like that, you think they can't be serious, that no one could be so evil, so despicable. But they were sincere, this pair of bloodthirsty brothers.

"What is it you want?" I asked as Blue Water Woman came out of the trees carrying firewood.

"I would like to know the same thing," she said.

Cutter, who was a few feet behind her, growled, "Shut up and start the fire. We will say when you can talk."

"Now, now," Jess Hook said. "She has a right to know. After all, whether she lives or dies depends on how it works out."

"What are you talking about?" I yearned to jump up and smash him in the face with my fist, but he and his brother wisely stood far enough back that I could not reach them before I was shot.

"We want their gold," Jess said.

Blue Water Woman was hunkering to deposit the firewood. "That again," she said. "You have gone to a lot of trouble for nothing. There is no gold and never was."

Cutter drew his knife partway and took a menacing step toward her. "Don't lie to us, squaw. We heard about the gold nugget your husband flashed at Bent's Fort."

"And where there's one nugget there are more," Jess Hook said. He practically glowed with greed. "We want to know where."

"I speak with a straight tongue when I say there never was more than the one nugget my husband had."

"You are lying to save your skin," Jordy Hook said. "We've heard all the stories about the strike you and the Kings made."

"If we had gold, don't you think we would have used more of it than one nugget?" Blue Water Woman responded.

Without any hint of what he was about to do, Jordy shoved her so hard she fell onto her hands and knees.

I started to rise to go to her when Jess Hook took a quick step and rammed the barrel of his rifle into my gut. The pain was terrible. I doubled over, my teeth grit, and could not help but groan.

"Stay right where you are, fancy pants."

I managed to croak, "You will pay for this!" Then I sucked air into my lungs, struggling to compose myself.

"You better keep one thing in mind, mister. Because make no mistake. My brother or me or Cutter will kill you and this squaw dead as dead can be if we have to, and not feel a twinge of regret after the deed is done."

"Regret, hell," Cutter said. "Me, I *like* to kill, and have ever since I was twelve and took a pitchfork to my pa. He had a habit of slapping me around when I gave him sass."

Blue Water Woman had calmly picked herself up and resumed kindling a fire. She did not curse Cutter or even glare at him.

I marveled at her self-control. My own was not nearly as superb. When I could sit up straight, I asked, "How do you propose to get your hands on this gold that doesn't exist?"

"That is where you and this squaw come in. I will tell you all about it once we have a fire going and coffee on."

I could think of nothing else to say beyond a few choice comments about their character and intelligence, but insults were bound to earn me more pain so I sat in a funk until flames crackled and the aroma of brewing coffee filled the air.

I sat close to Blue Water Woman, inwardly resolved to leap to her aid if they tried to hurt her again. Jess Hook sat across from us. His brother and Cutter stood well back, Cutter near the horses, so they could thwart any escape attempt.

"Now then," Jess said with that mocking smile of his, "suppose we get down to business. We want the gold, but we're willing to be reasonable."

"You call *this* reasonable?" I said sarcastically.

"So long as you and the squaw get to go on breathing, I would say so, yes."

"Do not call me that," Blue Water Woman said softly. Jess glanced at her. "What did you say?"

"Do not call me squaw. I have a name."

"So what if you do? To us you are nothing but a stinking redskin. We will call you whatever we damn well please, and you'll keep your mouth shut." Jess waited for her to reply. She didn't. He grinned and said, "Now then, where were we?" He turned to me. "It's simple, really. The squaw stays with us while you ride down and tell her husband and the Kings to hand over the gold or they will never set eyes on her again."

I had suspected something like this. "You are despicable."

"Keep giving me guff, fancy pants," Jess said, "and you'll have to do your riding with a broken finger or two. Do you want that?"

I did not.

"Good. Then in a bit you will head out. Cutter will follow you to make sure you go straight to the lake. Try anything, and we kill the squaw. If her husband or the Kings try anything, we kill the squaw. Make it plain to them. If there's so much as a whiff of trouble, we kill the squaw."

"I daresay if you harm her, Shakespeare McNair and Nate King will not rest until they have hunted you down and exacted their vengeance."

"They don't scare us none," Jess said. "McNair is tough, but he's as old as Methuselah. And so what if Nate King has killed a lot of grizzlies? Bears don't shoot back."

His brother chuckled.

"Tell them they are to load the gold onto packhorses, and then you are to bring it up to us."

"Why me?" I asked.

"Because you're harmless."

I have been insulted before, but that one caused me to burn with resentment. I was on the verge of saying something that would undoubtedly anger him when Blue Water Woman cleared her throat.

"May I speak?"

"Sure, squaw," Jess Hook said. "What is on your mind?"

"Why involve my husband and the Kings when there is no need?"

"You know a better way?"

"I will take you to the gold myself."

"What?"

"You have been right all along," Blue Water Woman said. "There is gold, and plenty of it."

Chapter Fourteen

I was stunned. I had believed her when she said there wasn't any gold. Now to find out she had lied crushed the esteem in which I held her.

"My husband and I only have enough to fill a parfleche," Blue Water Woman was saying. "But I can take you to where he found it. I can show you the vein. You can dig out all you want. Enough to make all of you wealthy. What do you say?"

Jess Hook's eyes narrowed suspiciously. "Why so generous all of a sudden? Why the change of heart?"

"I do not want my husband harmed. If he finds out you have me, he might try to save me. But if I show you the vein, we can keep him out of this."

"That makes sense," Jordy Hook said.

"I have two conditions," Blue Water Woman informed them. "The first is that once you have your gold, Robert Parker and I are to be set free."

Jess smirked. "Like I said, I can be reasonable. What is the second?"

"As I asked you before, that you stop calling me squaw. To me that is an insult. Either use my name or do not call me anything."

Cutter started toward her, growling, "Uppity red bitch."

"Now, now," Jess said, holding up a hand. "Let her be. She's making things easy for us, so it won't hurt us to go easy on her."

Jordy Hook said, "It won't kill you to be nice until we get there."

Cutter stopped, but he was not happy. "Exactly how long will it take, anyhow?"

"Good question." Jess looked at Blue Water Woman.

"Five days," she said.

"It's not somewhere close?"

Blue Water Woman extended a finger toward the south end of the valley. "The vein is high on a mountain, at the base of a cliff."

"And how did your husband find it?" Jess asked. He did not sound convinced.

"He was searching for signs of a pass. We found one to the west and Nate King set off a keg of powder to close it."

"Why in hell would he do that?"

"So anyone who might harm us cannot enter our valley without us being aware. We want only the one way in and out."

"Have you seen this vein with your own eyes?" Jess asked.

Blue Water Woman nodded. "The gold is mixed with quartz, but there is more gold than quartz"

"How much, would you say?"

"I do not know how far in the veins goes," Blue Water Woman said. "But one band of yellow is as long as I am tall, and as wide as this coffeepot."

"Sweet Jesus!" Jordy exclaimed.

"We'll be richer than John Jacob Aster," Jess said.

Cutter cursed and glanced sourly at each of the

brothers in turn. "Lunkheads. I am partnered with lunkheads. So what if she shows us the vein? How do we dig the gold out? With our fingers?"

Jess stiffened. "I hadn't thought of that."

"Set your minds at ease," Blue Water Woman said. "My husband did not want to keep taking his tools back and forth so he cached them near the vein. A pick and shovel and other things."

"Perfect!" Jordy declared. "Just perfect!"

"Too perfect, if you ask me," Cutter remarked.

"Listen to yourself," Jess Hook said. "Our wish is about to come true and all you do is gripe. What good would it do her to lie when she knows what we would do to her and Parker?"

"I'm just saying we shouldn't trust her until we see the gold ourselves," Cutter said.

"That goes without saying. Now simmer down, will you? Five days from now we'll be the happiest gents alive. If it turns out she's lying, we'll just go back to our original plan."

"Let's head out as soon as we have had some coffee," Jordy proposed. "The sooner we start, the sooner we get there."

Blue Water Woman poured when the coffee was ready. The brothers joked and laughed. Cutter, though, was in a foul temper, and no amount of friendly coaxing by the Hooks could change his mood.

For my own part, I was depressed. I was disappointed in Blue Water Woman, disgusted with our captors, and dismayed that I would not be able to paint or sketch until our ordeal was over. Or would I? I put the question to Jess Hook, who blinked and regarded me as he might a snake with wings.

"Don't you beat all."

"I'm sorry?"

"Your life is at stake, and all you can think of is the silly work you do?" Jess chortled. "Sure, mister, sure. You can draw and paint, so long as you behave. But mind you, We'll be in the saddle most of the time, and we're not stopping just so you can draw some bird or bug."

"What sort of man are you?" Jordy Hook asked me. "Playing with brushes is not fit for a grown-up."

His absurdity angered me. "What are you talking about? The work I do is for science. For expanding the boundaries of human knowledge."

Jess Hook whistled. "Listen to you! You never use a small word when a big one will do, huh?"

"I am only saying naturalists are important."

Jordy said, "You can puff yourself up as much as you want, but I know silly when I see it and what you do is plumb silly."

I have often wondered how some people can be so dense between the ears. Granted, no two minds are alike, and granted, just as there are sharp razors and dull razors, so, too, are there sharp minds and dull minds. But honestly. How mental sluggards like Jordy Hook can remember to take their next breath is beyond me.

If that seems harsh, it is only because I have been teased before about my profession. People look at me askance, as if cataloging the creatures we share this planet with suggests I am crazy. One fellow of my acquaintance referred to me as "that guy who chases butterflies." Another once called me, and I quote, "the loon who likes animals more than people."

In any event, the rest of that afternoon was a blur. I was lost inside myself, and except for having to tug on the rope to my packhorse now and again, I was oblivious to the world around me.

I did vaguely note that we were giving the valley floor a wide berth, and staying high enough up and in heavy enough timber that it was unlikely anyone would spot us, even through a spyglass.

Their dull intellects notwithstanding, the Hook brothers were cautious and clever.

Toward sunset we stopped for the night. Blue Water Woman was told to cook a rabbit Cutter killed with a knife. I saw him do it, and I cannot quite believe what I saw. We were in among spruce when the rabbit bolted from cover. It took a few bounds and then, perhaps out of curiosity, stopped to stare at us.

Cutter was the last in line, and it so happened that the rabbit stopped near him. His hand moved, and metal gleamed in the sun, all so fast that had I blinked I would have missed it. The rabbit leaped high into the air, a knife stuck in its side. It kicked convulsively, then was still.

I was impressed. Considerable skill is required to throw a knife with speed and accuracy.

Now, sitting by the fire and watching the rabbit slowly roast on a spit, I wrapped my arms around my knees and racked my brain for a way out of our predicament. The Hook brothers and Cutter were over by the horses, talking in low tones. About us, I guessed. Venting a sigh, I remarked to Blue Water Woman, "This is a fine mess we are in."

"Those are the first words you have said to me since noon. I thought you had lost the power of speech."

"How can you make light of our plight?" I responded. "We are in the company of killers, pawns to their every whim."

"It is worse than you think."

"That is not possible," I assured her. "The only thing worse would be if we were dead."

Blue Water Woman leaned toward me and whispered, "There is no gold, Robert."

"What?"

"I lied. There is no cliff, no vein, no gold."

I was dumbfounded.

"Are you all right?"

It was all I could do to keep my voice down. "Do you realize what you have done? Do you know how mad those three will be? They will slit our throats for sure."

"They intend to anyway," Blue Water Woman said. "They have no intention of letting us go."

"Why the charade? What do you hope to gain?"

"Five days of life. Five days in which, as you whites say, to turn the tables. Five days in which we must do to them as they plan to do to us."

That gave me pause. "Wait a minute. Are you suggesting *we* kill *them*?"

"If we do not, we are dead. And I very much enjoy being alive." Blue Water Woman reached over and placed a hand on my leg. "Understand this, Robert. It is us or them."

"You expect too much of me," I said. "I have never killed anyone. I don't know as I can. Frankly, it amazes me that anyone can take another human life."

She studied me, then said, "When I was a child, our village was raided. More than once. I saw the bodies of people I cared for. I saw an uncle who had been gutted, and his intestines hanging out. I saw a girl, a close friend, whose head had been bashed in with a war club. I stood over her and watched as her brains oozed out."

"We come from different worlds," I remarked.

"There is more. Among my people, the men are the fighters, the warriors. But Salish women are expected to fight, too, when the need arises. When our villages are attacked, the women resist fiercely."

I surmised what she was leading to. "You have killed before then, I take it?"

"Only when I had to. The first time, I was eleven—"

"Dear Lord."

"—a Piegan had my brother on the ground and was about to stab him when I ran up and plunged a knife into the Piegan's neck. I can still feel his blood on my hand and arm, still see his eyes widen and hear his gasps."

"I could not do that."

"I need to know I can count on you, Robert. I cannot best all three of them alone." Blue Water Woman gave a barely perceptible nod at our captors, then whispered, "Will you help, Robert? Are you with me?"

I looked into her eyes and would have agreed to anything. Swallowing, I said, "I am with you to the extent that I will do what I can to help. But I do not think I can do the actual killing."

"Leave that to me, then," Blue Water Woman said. "When it happens, it will happen fast. So be ready." She had more to say, but just then the brothers came over to the fire.

"What are you two jabbering about?" Jess Hook asked.

"Our plight," I said. "And how happy we will be after she shows you the gold and you let us go." I said it to test his reaction, closely watching his face as I did, and for the briefest of instants I saw in his eyes that Blue Water Woman was right; they had no intention of permitting us to go free.

I assumed Blue Water Woman would wait a day or two before she made her bid to escape. That is what I would do. I would lull them into thinking I was going along with them, and catch them when their guard was down.

Even so, I spent the evening in a state of nervous expectation. The rabbit was delicious, but I did not eat much. After our meal, the brothers and Cutter sat and talked about their previous escapades. Although "escapades" does not do their evil natures justice. They casually mentioned people they had killed and laughed about gruesome deeds they had committed.

At one point Jess said, "Do you remember that family in the wagon? The settlers who aimed to build a cabin in the foothills?"

Jordy chuckled. "The husband sure was a trusting soul. The look on his face when Cutter stuck him!"

Cutter's cruel features curled in one of his rare grins. "I got him low down, and he squealed like a stuck pig. It took the yack a long time to die."

Is it any wonder my thoughts turned to the dark depths to which a perverse soul may sink? I slept fitfully, tossing and turning, and must have woken up half a dozen times.

Toward dawn my eyes suddenly opened. I lay on my back, staring up at the stars and contemplating the fickle nature of fate. It depressed me, so I rolled onto my side to try and get back to sleep.

For a few seconds I could not make sense of what I was seeing.

Jess Hook and Cutter were snoring. Jordy Hook was supposed to be keeping watch. He was seated by the fire, which had dwindled to tiny flames, his forehead on his knee, his rifle by his side. He had dozed off.

An arm's length from him, on her belly, was Blue Water Woman. As I set eyes on her, she slid one arm forward, then a leg.

She was not waiting a day or two.

She was making her bid now.

My insides churned. If Jordy or one of the others woke up, there was no telling what they would do to her.

Blue Water Woman inched forward. She was close enough now to touch him. Her hand snaked toward the knife on Jordy's hip. He mumbled in his sleep, and she froze. When he stopped, she extended her arm all the way and lightly grasped the hilt.

I scarcely breathed. I glanced at Jess and Cutter. They slept on, undisturbed.

Blue Water Woman started to ease the knife from its sheath. She had it almost out when that which I feared most, occurred.

Jordy Hook grunted, opened his eyes and sat up.

Chapter Fifteen

Some moments we never forget. They are indelibly seared into our memories. When we think of them, they are as fresh as when they happened.

This was one of those moments for me. I thought for sure Jordy would yell and the others would leap up, with dire consequences.

But quick as lightning, Blue Water Woman drew his knife and plunged it into his ribs. Jordy's back arched and his mouth opened. She clamped her other hand over his lips before he could yell, and like a punctured water skin he deflated and sank onto his side on top of his rifle. She tugged at the weapon, but it would not come free. She snatched one of his pistols instead. Then, yanking the knife out and beckoning to me, she rose into a crouch and moved toward the horses.

I was on my feet and at her heels in a twinkling. I was stunned, my mind sluggish. We were halfway to the string when I realized that if we rode off, I would have to leave my journal, paintings and sketches behind. I could not do that. I stopped.

Blue Water Woman reached the first horse. She glanced back, and motioned.

I shook my head. I refused to leave my work in the hands of cutthroats who might destroy it.

She motioned a second time, urgently.

I had to make her understand. I hurried toward her to explain.

That was when the horse, apparently smelling the blood on the knife, whinnied.

Jess Hook rose onto his elbows. He saw his brother. He saw us. His hand swooped to his pistols and he roared, "Cutter! They're trying to get away!"

Fingers wrapped around my arm, and I was pulled bodily into the dark. I did not resist. Too much was happening too fast.

A flintlock boomed and lead buzzed past my ear. Suddenly my life took precedence over my work, and when Blue Water Woman broke into a run, so did I. Fortunately, she retained her grip on my arm. It was pitch-black in the forest, and I could barely see her. Trees and other objects streaked by. How she managed, I can't say.

The crackle of underbrush warned me of pursuit. From the sounds, only one of them was after us. I suspected it was Cutter. Jess would be checking Jordy; his rage would be boundless.

Blue Water Woman was uncanny. She threaded swiftly through the trees, avoiding obstacles with a facility that made me marvel. And she did so while making no more noise than a wraith. I wish I could say the same, but compared to her, I was a blundering ox.

I stepped on a dry twig. At the crunch, the night behind us flared with thunder and a tree I was passing thudded to the impact of a slug. I ran faster.

Soon we came to a slope and started down. I was running blind, relying completely on Blue Water Woman.

A sudden blow to the forehead rocked me on my heels. I had blundered into a low tree limb. Everything spun. My knees were wobbly. I staggered and groped for Blue Water Woman. Her hands found my arm, and she pulled me down to the ground and placed a palm over my mouth. Her warm lips brushed my ear.

"Be still, Robert."

Cutter was crashing toward us. Apparently he had thrown stealth to the wind. The crashing stopped about fifteen feet away, and I spied his silhouette. He cursed and turned right and left.

He had lost us!

From the camp came a shout.

"Cutter! Get back here! Jordy's hurt bad! I need your help right away!"

Swearing anew, Cutter wheeled and flew back up the mountain.

I was both elated and vexed. Elated that we had gotten away but vexed at leaving my work, which was everything to me. I was also disturbed that Jordy still lived.

Blue Water Woman did not move. I was growing impatient when she at last whispered in my ear, "We can go on."

"You, not me," I said.

Her face loomed so near that our noses practically touched. "What are you saying, Robert?"

"I can't leave my work. All I have gone through will have been in vain."

"You cannot go back. They will kill you."

"Maybe not," I said hopefully. "But it is a risk I must take. In the meantime, fetch your husband and the Kings." I started to stand, but she still had hold of my arm and did not let go. "Release me, if you please."

"I cannot let you do this."

"Don't worry about me," I said. "The important thing is that you are safe." Even more important were the fruits of my weeks of labor, but I did not come right out and say that.

"When I said I cannot let you, I meant it." So saying, Blue Water Woman pressed the tip of the blade against the back of my right hand. A sharp pain shot up my arm. I tried to recoil but she held me fast.

"What in God's name are you doing?" I demanded.

"You are coming with me whether you want to or not. Refuse, and you will never paint another animal or make another entry in your journal unless you learn to do so with your other hand."

Her meaning was clear. "You wouldn't!"

"I will save you however I must."

"It is my decision to make, not yours. You have no right to force me against my will."

"I will not have your death on my conscience." Without taking the tip of the knife from my hand, Blue Water Woman pulled me to my feet and we resumed our flight.

I was horror-struck. One misstep, and the blade would slice into my hand, severing tendons and nerves.

Gradually, my horror gave way to simmering fury. We had gone about two hundred yards and I had lost sight of the campfire when I drew up short. "Take that knife away this instant."

"Will you stay with me if I do?"

"Are all the Salish so stubborn?" I rejoined.

"We do not let those we care for die for no reason."

I submitted, partly because I was touched by her concern and partly because I doubted my ability to find my way back in the dark. Still, I fretted with every step that took me farther from that which meant so much to me. Some might deem it foolish, but consider that it would be impossible for me to reproduce the paintings and sketches. Oh, I might render other animals and plants of the same kind, but I did not have canvas and paper to squander, and the sum of my work would be that much less.

"I am sorry I had to do this, Robert," Blue Water Woman said as she finally lowered the knife.

"Don't seek to make amends," I said bitterly. "You don't realize what this could cost me."

"Which is more valuable, your work or your life?"

"I measure the one by the other. My work defines who I am. It will endure long after I am gone."

"Your outlook is peculiar," Blue Water Woman said, glancing over her shoulder. She grinned. "Even for a white man."

"On the contrary," I said. "Many whites measure their worth by what they do and not who they are or how much they have."

"Are they as serious as you? Do they ever relax and savor being alive? Or have they forgotten there is more to life than work?"

"I have not reached that point," I said defensively. Or had I? Ever since I crossed the Mississippi River, I had become obsessed. But who could blame me, what with the bounty of new species to be recorded and the possibility of a position at a prestigious university?

We fell silent after that. Blue Water Woman moved so rapidly, I soon tired.

"Is it necessary we walk ourselves into the ground?"

"The sun waits for no one," Blue Water Woman responded, and gestured at the eastern horizon.

A rosy glow presaged the dawn.

"How soon do you expect them to come after us?" I asked.

"As soon as it is light enough."

I prayed she was wrong. They had horses. They would swiftly overtake us, and unless we were very lucky or very crafty, or both, we would again find ourselves their captives.

It was incentive to keep up with my liberator.

Suddenly I was struck by a thought. I was the man, yet she was saving us. Was I so puny that I needed a woman to rescue me? Yes, I am a naturalist, not a frontiersman or a soldier or a law officer, and my wilderness skills were laughable. But was that sufficient reason to let her take charge?

I decided it was. I was perfectly content to let her handle things. The arrogance that causes men to treat women as inferior, I can proudly state, is not one of my faults.

Degree by degree the sky was brightening. The sun had not appeared but the whole of the eastern sky was pink and orange. Some people say that sunrises never rival sunsets, but I have seen my share of dawns, and they can be as spectacular.

A bird warbled. As if that were a signal, a legion of others broke out in song.

Blue Water Woman stopped and cocked her head, listening. "They come," she announced.

I did not hear them, but I took her word for it. We ran to a thicket and she dropped onto all fours and crawled in among the brambles, urging me to stay close to her. Not so easily done, what with the sharp tips of the branches threatening to poke out my eyes. We went forty or fifty feet and then were up and running, the thicket behind us, pines ahead. I sensed she was making for a specific spot and soon she proved me right. The vegetation thinned and we came to a stop on the bank of a stream.

"Wade in," Blue Water Woman said, doing so.

"I know this trick," I told her. "Zach used it to try and shake the Hooks and Cutter off our trail." I added, "It didn't work."

"Let us hope we have more success."

Sticking to the middle, Blue Water Woman headed downstream. She did not hike her dress as many white women would do.

The water was cold. I was soon soaked to near my knees. A stiff breeze from high up the mountain added to my discomfort.

Neither the water nor the wind seemed to have any effect on Blue Water Woman. She was made of iron.

In due course the sun poked over the rim of the world. The forest was alive with birds, and other small creatures were stirring after their night of rest.

"No sign of pursuit yet," I said.

"They will come," Blue Water Woman declared.

I wanted to keep talking. It took my mind off how cold I was, and my empty stomach, and my paintings and my journal. So I gave voice to the first thing that popped into my head. "Do you ever regret marrying a white man?"

Blue Water Woman broke stride and glanced back at me. "A strange thing to ask at a time like this." She moved on.

"Zach King told me that a lot of whites and Indians look down their noses at those who wed outside their own kind."

"I do not care what others think. I do not care what they say. I live my life as I want and not as they want."

"You are happy, then?"

"Happy beyond words, Robert Parker. Shakespeare is a special man, and I am honored he loves me."

"Have you ever wished Shakespeare and you had children?"

Blue Water Woman was quiet a bit, then she said, "It is my one great sadness."

"Forgive me for asking."

"When a woman loves a man, she desires to please him every way she can. I know Shakespeare dearly desired a family, and I yearned to give him one. But it was not meant to be." She paused. "Perhaps it is just as well. We married late in life. It is hard when you are old to keep up with the young."

Despite their years, I did not think of them as old. "I hope to heaven I have half his vitality when I am his age. Or yours, for that matter." She moved with a supple grace I found enticing.

"My husband likes to say we are as old as we think we are," Blue Water Woman mentioned. "When he has lived one hundred winters, I imagine he will behave as if he has lived fifteen."

I chuckled.

"But to answer your question, no, I do not regret taking him for my mate. I love him, and I will go on loving him with all that I am until the day I die."

At that instant I would gladly have pushed Shakespeare McNair off a cliff. But I settled for saying, "He is fortunate."

Blue Water Woman glanced back at me again. "Tell him what I told you, Robert, if something should happen to me."

"Don't talk like that," I said. Intimations of death crept over me, but I shrugged them off. Nerves, I decided. Nothing but nerves.

"We all die."

"Yes, but we need not die *today*."

"The time and place is not always ours to decide."

I was uncomfortable talking about it. "Perhaps you are mistaken. Perhaps they won't come after us, and the rest of the day will be uneventful."

Hardly was the statement out of my mouth when we rounded a bend and Blue Water Woman drew up so abruptly, I nearly walked into her.

"What is it?" I asked, stepping to one side to see what she was seeing.

"Stand still!"

On our left was a bank, approximately shoulder height. And crouched on the bank was a mountain lion.

Chapter Sixteen

I had never seen a mountain lion up close. I knew they were big, but I never thought they were *this* big. The specimen crouched on the bank was almost ten feet from the tip of its nose to the end of its tail, and had to weigh close to three hundred pounds. The upper part of its body was a tawny hue bordering on gray; below, the chest and underside were white. It had a broad nose and piercing yellow eyes. Dark patches on both sides of its mouth accented its whiskers.

Even though it was poised to spring, I was not especially afraid. I knew of only a few instances where cougars attacked humans. Usually, they ran off.

Blue Water Woman extended her pistol, but she did not shoot, which was wise in my estimation since she could not be certain of killing it.

Then a rumbling growl issued from the giant cat's throat, and it bared its formidable fangs.

Fear spiked through me. Mountain lions are incredibly strong and inhumanly swift. What with their teeth and their claws, they can shred flesh to ribbons. Should this one spring, our lives might be forfeit.

Blue Water Woman sidled to the left so she was between the mountain lion and me. "I will hold it off as long as I can, Robert. Run and keep running until you are sure it is not after you."

Her willingness to sacrifice her life to save mine moved me deeply. "What sort of man do you take me for?"

"A smart one," Blue Water Woman said.

"I will not desert you, come what may." The idea was preposterous. I might not be much of a protector, but I would do what I could.

The mountain lion snarled, its long tail twitching. The sinews on its powerful legs stood out as it prepared to leap.

Of all the ways to die, this would be extremely unpleasant. I cast about for a good-sized rock or something else to use was a weapon, and when I glanced at the mountain lion again, it had uncoiled slightly and was staring up the mountain, not at us. The next instant it whirled and bounded into the forest, a tawny streak that was gone in the blink of an eye.

"What on earth?" I said.

Blue Water Woman turned, then bobbed her chin. "I told you, Robert. As soon as it was light enough."

Riders had appeared. Three of them, not two, threading through the trees. They were too far off to notice features, but it could only be our pursuers.

"Jordy, too?" I had hoped he was dead.

"I stabbed at his heart, but the blade glanced off a rib," Blue Water Woman said.

They had not seen us yet. All three were scouring the ground for tracks, the Hook brothers on one side of the stream, Cutter on the other.

Blue Water Woman's hand found mine. "We must be quick, Robert."

We continued down the middle of the stream. Another bend temporarily hid us. I was anxious to seek concealment, but she kept going, glancing right and left. I did not appreciate why until we came to a gravel bar.

"Step where I do," Blue Water Woman said.

The gravel bar was covered with small stones and did not yield to my weight. I understood immediately. Except for the wet imprint of our soles, which would soon dry, we did not leave tracks. Crouching low so as not to be seen from above, I followed her into the woods.

Our enemies were a quarter of a mile above us, still paralleling the stream.

"We must find a spot to make our stand," Blue Water Woman proposed.

"Maybe they will go on by," I said.

"They will find us. Come." Blue Water Woman ran to the north.

I wondered how we were to fight three well-armed killers when all we had was a knife and pistol. I did not say anything, though. After we had gone a few hundred feet we came on a low bluff.

Blue Water Woman stopped. "This will do nicely."

Approximately twenty feet high and twice that long, the bluff was an isolated island in a sea of trees, mainly spruce and pines. The side facing us was sheer, but the crest could be reached by slopes on either side.

Blue Water Woman jogged to the right and took the slope at a run. I was puffing for breath when I caught up to her.

"Why here?" I gasped.

"I have a clear shot," Blue Water Woman replied. "Then it will be two against two."

"Once you fire, your pistol will be useless," I mentioned. "What about the two you don't shoot?"

Blue Water Woman nudged a fist-sized rock with her toe. "We will use what is handy."

"Rocks against bullets?"

She faced me and her expression grew severe. "Listen to me, Robert. Listen closely. They plan to kill us. Whether now or later, our end will be the same. We must fight or we will die."

"I understand that," I said rather testily. I did not like being treated as if I were a simpleton.

"Do you truly?" Blue Water Woman persisted. "Because you seem to think it is silly of us to fight for our lives when we have so little chance of beating them. Or am I mistaken?"

I opened my mouth to tell her she definitely was—then closed it again when I realized she definitely wasn't.

"I thought so." Blue Water Woman placed her hand—the hand holding the bloody knife—on my shoulder. "I cannot do this alone, Robert. We must work together."

I answered her honestly. "I told you before I will do what I can."

Blue Water Woman squeezed my shoulder. "Very well. We must be true to our natures. I want you to go now."

"What?"

"I want you to go," she repeated. "You can be of little help to me, and I do not want you to die."

"I told you I would not desert you."

"Please, Robert," Blue Water Woman said. "I cannot devote attention to you when they come. You would be on your own." She smiled, not a mocking smile but a smile of genuine affection that cut me to my core. "I believe the white expression is that you would not stand a prayer."

"I am staying and that is final."

"Oh, Robert." Blue Water Woman frowned, but she did not press the issue. She stepped to the rim.

"Tell me what to do and I will do it," I said.

"I already did."

"I will do anything but abandon you. There must be something. I am not totally worthless."

"There is nothing you—" Blue Water Woman said, and caught herself. She glanced at me, her brow knit. "Your talent for making what you see so lifelike on canvas and paper. Can you do the same without a brush or pencil?"

"I am not sure I follow you."

Blue Water Woman tugged at my jacket, then pointed at the trees below the bluff and to the right. "If you do it so they think it is you, it will give us a slight edge."

I caught on and started down. "I will do you proud."

"Robert?"

I looked back.

"Stay down there. When the moment is right, yell."

"How will I know when that is?"

"You will know." Blue Water Woman rose onto the tips of her toes and gazed in the direction of the stream. "We have five minutes, Robert. Less, perhaps."

I ran. I chose a spruce near the bluff. Removing my jacket, I roved in search of downed limbs. The first branch I found had been on the ground so long it fell apart when I picked it up. The next branch was too thin. The third was too short. The fourth did not have leaves or offshoots. At last I found one that was suitable.

There were problems. How was I to replicate my head, for instance? Or my legs? Stripping off my jacket, I draped it around the leafy half of the branch.

Then I jabbed the jagged end into the ground. It penetrated, but not deep enough for the limb to stay upright on its own. I jabbed and poked some more, but the ground was too hard. My only recourse was to lean the branch against the tree. I contrived to place it so that one shoulder, part of the front, and a sleeve were visible. I tucked the end of the sleeve into a pocket and stepped back.

At a quick glance, it would pass for someone standing behind the spruce.

"I see them, Robert!"

Blue Water Woman had flattened. She motioned for me to seek cover and then slid back out of sight.

Darting behind a pine a few feet away, I dropped onto my stomach. Every nerve tingled. I was scared, terribly scared, yet at the same time I was excited. Silly, I know. But that was how I felt.

Only then did it occur to me that I did not have a weapon. I glanced around and saw a rock about the size of a small melon. I hefted it. It was heavy, but I could throw it if I had to.

A faint drumming heralded their approach.

I sucked in a deep breath and pressed against the earth. My heart pounded and there was a roaring in my ears. Then the roaring faded, and I could hear the horses clearly. They were coming on fast.

The irony did not escape me. Here I was, a man of peaceful pursuits, about to engage in violence.

How do things like this happen? How can it be that we go through life minding our own business, wanting only to live as we please without hindrance, yet find ourselves at risk through no fault of our own? I am no pastor or philosopher, but it seems to me that our Maker has a cruel sense of humor.

These were the musings that ran through my mind

as the hoofbeats swelled in volume, until all of a sudden the undergrowth crackled, and into the clear space below the bluff trotted Jess and Jordy Hook and their vicious friend, Cutter. They promptly drew rein.

Jordy Hook was not wearing a shirt. Bandages consisting of strips of buckskin had been crudely wrapped around the lower half of his chest. They were stained red with dry blood. He held a rifle, which he wagged excitedly. "They can't be far! One of us should circle around in front of them so we catch them between us."

"We stick together," Jess Hook said. He was staring at the top of the bluff, as if he suspected something.

None of them noticed the branch with my jacket on it poking from behind the spruce.

I was in a quandary. Blue Water Woman had said I would know when the time was right to distract them. But I did not know whether to do it then or wait. If I waited too long, they would ride off. What was I to do?

"Let's keep going," Jordy Hook urged. "I want them, brother. I want to break their bones and cut them. I want them to suffer until they scream."

"We should rest the horses," Cutter suggested. "We have pushed them hard and they are tuckered out."

"To hell with the horses!" Jordy fumed. "That squaw stabbed me! I won't rest until I have paid her back in kind."

"Cutter has a point," Jess said. "We can spare five minutes."

I gnawed on my lower lip in worry. Any second, they were bound to spot the jacket.

"I am not waiting!" Jordy bellowed. "I will stop when we catch them and not before."

"It is stupid to ride your animal into the ground," Cutter said.

Jordy flushed with resentment. "Since when did you give a damn about our animals or anything else?"

"Be careful," Cutter said.

"Or what? You will turn on me? You don't scare me, Harold. I've killed as many as you."

I peeked out at them. Did he just say Cutter's real name was *Harold*?

"You are acting like a ten-year-old," Cutter said. "But then, that is nothing new. Your brother was always more mature."

Jess Hook reined his horse between them. "Enough! This bickering ends now. We're partners, damn it. We must work together and cover each other's backs."

"Tell that to your brother," Cutter said.

Their rancor was a welcome development. I half hoped Jordy would shoot Cutter to spite him.

"When I said enough, I meant it!" Jess Hook snapped. "This squabbling is senseless."

"All right, all right," Cutter responded.

Jess glanced at Jordy who was so mad he was fit to fly out of his saddle at Cutter. "And what about you? Forgive and forget?"

"When hell freezes over. He called me stupid and a ten-year-old. You heard him."

"You've been called worse." Jess tiredly ran a sleeve across his brow. "We must keep our wits about us, brother. It is not deer we hunt."

"A squaw and a puny yack," Jordy said. "They don't stand a chance."

"Tell that to the knife she stuck in you."

"You can go to hell, too," Jordy said.

"Now you're picking a fight with me?" Jess said. "The one person in this world who gives a damn about you?"

"I'm mad at him, not you."

I was so intent on the two of them that I did not see Cutter gaze in the direction of the spruce. The first intimation I had that he had noticed the jacket was when he jerked his rifle up.

"Over there! Look!"

The next moment Cutter gigged his horse toward the spruce—and me.

Chapter Seventeen

I lay frozen in surprise.

Jess and Jordy raised their reins, Jordy bellowing, "Don't you kill him! I want him to die slow!"

Cutter had snapped his rifle to his shoulder, but he did not shoot. His eyes narrowed and he exclaimed, "What the hell?"

Suddenly Blue Water Woman's head and shoulders were silhouetted against the blue of the sky. She aimed the pistol at the closest to her, who happened to be Jordy. It spat smoke and lead, and at the crack of the shot, Jordy threw his arms into the air and slumped forward over his mount.

"Jordy!" Jess cried, reining around.

Cutter glanced back, and drew rein.

My body moved without my brain willing it to. I was on my feet, my arm cocked to throw the rock, before I quite knew what I was doing. I threw it with all my might, and much to my amazement, my throw was true.

The rock caught Cutter in the temple, and he reeled in the saddle and nearly fell.

Jess seized hold of the reins to his brother's mount and galloped to the south. Another instant, and Cutter, still reeling, raced after them.

I whooped for joy and broke from cover. I felt much as David must have felt when he slew Goliath.

Blue Water Woman brought me down to earth. She came flying down the slope, shouting, "The rifle, Robert!"

Only then did I realize that Jordy had dropped his. I scooped it up and wheeled just as she reached me. Gladly giving it to her, I said happily, "We did it! We drove them off."

"They will be back, and we must not be here when they do." Blue Water Woman turned toward the valley floor so very far below, and once again we ran side by side.

"We have taught them not to take us lightly, at least," I said proudly. "And now there is one less."

"Perhaps," Blue Water Woman said.

"You hit him. I saw it."

"But did the slug strike his heart or a lung or miss his vitals altogether? We cannot take his death for granted."

"Either way, he will be in no shape to ride," I predicted. "And now that we have his rifle, the other two won't press us as hard." In my mind's eye I saw us reaching the cabins and rallying the Kings and McNair to track down the killers. We had as good as prevailed.

"You have a lot to learn about human nature, Robert," Blue Water Woman cautioned. "If Jordy does die, his brother will not rest until we have breathed our last."

"You are forgetting the vein of gold," I reminded her. "He won't harm us so long as he thinks you can lead him to it."

"I would not count on that overmuch were I you."

After that we had breath only for running. I did my best, but I slowed her down. She displayed the easy graceful lope of an antelope and could go forever without tiring. Me, I was hurting after a few hundred yards. But I doggedly ran on. I refused to let her be caught because of me.

We had descended for over an hour, with brief stops now and again so I could try to catch my breath, when we both heard the dreaded but familiar sound of hooves high above us.

Blue Water Woman stared up the mountain. "They took longer than I thought they would."

"We must find another spot to make a stand," I wheezed.

"This time we will try another trick."

Ahead were aspens. She made straight for them, I a puppy glued to her moccasins. The narrow boles were almost white in the bright sunlight. When she stopped, I was puzzled. Hardly any cover was to be had. The trees were too thin. "What are you up to?"

"This will do," Blue Water Woman said with a smile.

"For what? Our graves?"

She thrust the knife into my hand. "I will circle back on our trail to the right. You go to the left. Keep about ten paces from our tracks. Halfway to the spot where we entered the aspens, stop. Lie on your stomach and cover yourself with as many leaves as you can."

Her idea was brilliant. Our pursuers would be so intent on reading sign, they might not spot us.

"When they are close enough I will shoot one," Blue Water Woman said, "Then we will both rush whoever is left and end this."

I liked the shooting part; I did not like the rushing part. "But one of us is liable to take a slug."

"I will make as if I am reloading the rifle," Blue Water Woman said, "and keep the last one's attention on me. When you are close enough, stab him. Stab him again and again."

"If your plan works he will have his back to me."

"I will ask him to turn around so you can stab him in the chest."

"Your sarcasm is excellent, but I was not objecting," I said. "I will do what I have to. It is them or us, and I have grown fond of breathing."

"You are learning at last," Blue Water Woman said, and clapped me on the arm.

We set our trap. I did exactly as she told me. Plenty of leaves littered the ground, most of them dry and brittle. But by scooping carefully I did as she had directed. I could see her doing the same. She looked at me, and I smiled.

I envied Shakespeare McNair. Tavern gossip had it that Indian women made terrible wives. They were supposed to be smelly and dirty and little better than animals. I am here to record the opposite. Blue Water Woman was as much a lady as any white woman I ever met. She was intelligent, articulate and brave. She abhorred dirt. In short, she was as fine a female as I ever met. Yes, I envied Shakespeare McNair very much.

Her low cry drew me out of myself.

Two riders were nearing the aspens. Jess Hook and Cutter were abreast of each other, about thirty feet apart. The incident at the bluff had taught them a lesson. They rode primed for conflict, the stocks of their rifles on their thighs, their thumbs on the hammers and their fingers on the triggers.

Jordy was not with them. I suppose I should have been elated. But I experienced only the cold realization that we still had two cutthroats to deal with.

Ten yards from the aspens the pair drew rein.

Jess rose in the stirrups and scanned the stand from end to end. He was uneasy, and it showed.

"We can't sit here all day," Cutter complained.

"I just lost my only brother. We will sit here as long as I damn well please."

"I am only saying—" Cutter began.

"We should go around," Jess cut him off.

My breath caught in my throat. If they did that, and found no trace of us on the other side of the stand, they would know beyond any shadow of a doubt that we were hiding in it.

"There is such a thing as being too cautious," Cutter said.

"Ride on through if you want. Make it easy for them. Or have you forgotten they got their hands on Jordy's rifle?"

"I haven't forgotten," Cutter assured him, although were I a gambling man, I would wager he had.

"Whenever you're ready," Jess said.

I would not have done it for all the ivory in Africa. But then, I never pretend I am more than I am. I am a naturalist. I record new species for posterity. That is the sum and substance of my life.

Cutter poked his mount with his heels. He came slowly, scouring the aspens on both sides of him.

I imitated a log. The slightest movement would give me away. I refused even to blink.

"You are too pigheaded for your own good!" Jess called to Cutter, then reined to the right and headed around the stand.

Cutter did not answer. He was looking up in trees, behind trees, behind him. A distinct *click* warned me he had thumbed his rifle's hammer back.

My skin crawled. I was afraid if I twitched, he would blow the top of my head off.

Blue Water Woman was practically invisible. Her eyes and part of her face were all I could see and only because I knew where she was.

Jess Hook had goaded his mount to a gallop. He would not be a factor if we struck quickly. But Blue Water Woman did not shoot, not even when Cutter came abreast of us.

Inexplicably, Cutter stopped. I did not like how he was staring in my direction. I liked it even less when he shifted in the saddle and trained his rifle on me.

"You are a clever bastard. But that knife you are holding stands out clear as can be."

I had completely forgotten about it.

"On your feet, fancy pants, or I will kill you where you lie."

My legs did not want to cooperate, but I made it erect and stood with my arms at my sides. "You don't want to do this."

"Sure I do." Cutter laughed. "It was you who beaned me with that rock, wasn't it?" Without taking his eyes off me, he turned his head to display the discolored bump on his temple.

"I had to," I said. "You are out to kill us."

"Not then we weren't," Cutter said. "Jess and Jordy were hoping to take you and the squaw alive." He paused. "Where is she, anyhow? Where did that red bitch get to?"

"Right behind you," Blue Water Woman said. Her legs were visible under his horse on the other side.

Cutter stiffened and started to turn but reconsidered. A sly smile twisted his cruel mouth.

"I bet you have Jordy's rifle pointed at me, don't you?"

"You would win that bet," Blue Water Woman said. "And in case you are wondering, yes, I can shoot you in the back and not lose sleep over it."

I moved toward them, intending to disarm him. "Don't shoot. We will take him prisoner."

"No, Robert!" Blue Water Woman responded. "Stay back! This one is too dangerous."

I should have listened. But by then I was only a few steps from his horse, and I reached up to relieve him of his rifle. To my credit, I stepped to one side so I was not in front of the muzzle.

Cutter came out of the saddle like a bolt of lightning. In reflex I thrust the knife at him, but he swatted my forearm aside even as he slammed into me. His shoulder caught me full in the sternum, and I was smashed onto my back. I thought my chest would burst.

Cutter had let go of his rifle as he sprang, and now, straddling me, he whipped a pistol from under his belt and jammed the deadly end against my neck.

I did not understand why Blue Water Woman had not fired. Then I saw her over his shoulder; she rushed up and pointed the rifle at the back of his head. Whether her intention was to shoot or take him prisoner as I had requested was rendered moot by the click of his pistol. He glanced at her, showing his teeth in vicious glee.

"Go ahead, squaw. You shoot me and I shoot him. All it will take is a twitch of my finger."

Blue Water Woman hesitated.

"I thought so," Cutter crowed. "Drop the rifle and step around in front of me."

"Don't do it!" I cried.

Cutter, frowning, gouged the pistol into my neck. "Not another peep out of you."

I writhed in pain but dared not push at his arm for fear the pistol would go off.

Blue Water Woman was a study in indecision. My folly had placed us in a dreadful predicament. She could shoot him, but at the possible cost of my life. Our eyes met, and for a moment my pain was of no consequence. Then, reluctantly, she lowered her rifle, saying, "Very well. Do not kill him, and I will do as you say."

I was heart struck. She was sacrificing herself for my sake. This gentle woman whose friendship I valued so highly would lose her life because of my stupidity. I couldn't have that. I would not let her perish.

Cutter was looking at her, not at me. In his arrogance he had forgotten something; the knife I still held. He sneered at her, and I stabbed him in the belly.

I must say, the result was not what I expected. I thought he would collapse on top of me, dead, but I had no more luck stabbing him than Blue Water Woman did when she stabbed Jordy. Instead of collapsing, he roared like a wild beast and exploded into motion.

Cutter reared up off of me, hitting me with his pistol as he rose. Blue Water Woman tried to level her rifle, but he whirled and was on her in a bound. He swung the pistol and caught her above the ear. Down she went.

"No!" My head was spinning, but I heaved off the ground. "Get away from her, you slug!"

Cutter spun. He began to raise the pistol, then smiled and did the last thing I expected; he slid it under his belt. Not because he was giving up, but so he could draw one of his knives. He wagged it in a circle and said with relish, "I'm going to like doing you. You will die a hundred times before I am done."

"A person can only die once," I responded, struggling to clear my head. I was under no delusions. I was no match for him, none whatsoever.

As if the situation were not dire enough, hooves pounded and through the aspens came Jess Hook. He drew rein and aimed his rifle at me.

My time had come.

Chapter Eighteen

Life is a fickle mistress. She dispenses happiness and sadness with no regard for those under her sway. I had come to the Rockies for the sole purpose of expanding the horizons of human knowledge, yet my lofty goal counted for nothing when weighed in the balance by the scales of death. I was on the verge of being sent beyond the veil.

"No!" Cutter bellowed. "Don't you dare!"

Jess Hook did not lower his rifle, but he did look at Cutter and say in annoyance, "I have as much right as you. They killed my brother."

"She did!" Cutter said, pointing at Blue Water Woman's unconscious form. "Do what you want with her, but I do fancy pants here."

"Stop calling me that," I said.

Cutter's shirt was bloody, and scarlet drops were dripping over his belt and down his leg. "I mean it. Look at what he did to me. He's mine, and that's that."

Jess Hook straightened. "All right. The squaw is mine and he's yours. But we should take a look at you first. You're bleeding bad."

"I hardly feel it," Cutter said. "We'll look when I'm done with him and not before."

And just like that, he sprang.

I was not prepared. My head was still fuzzy and I was staring at Blue Water Woman, not at him. As it was, I evaded his knife only because I instinctively threw myself backward, and in doing so, tripped over my own feet. His blade cleaved air inches from my throat.

I landed on my back and scrambled away from him using my elbows and heels. Cutter came after me, slicing at my legs. I rolled to the right and pushed to my knees.

Cold steel arced toward my chest. I countered, and my knife rang on his. It jarred my arm to the bone.

Cutter was incensed. He redoubled his efforts, thrusting and slashing. I reacted without thinking and managed to block or avoid his blows. Suddenly he drew back, breathing heavily, which enabled me to get to my feet.

"Let me shoot him!" Jess Hook offered.

"No!" Cutter had his other hand pressed to his gut. The dark stain had spread and the top of his pants were now crimson.

"We'll tie him and you can kill him after I stitch you up!" Jess hollered.

"No," Cutter said again, and came at me in a fury.

How I stayed alive I will never know. His blade glittered and streaked. I dodged and ducked and danced to one side or the other. Self-preservation is a powerful instinct, and I attribute the fact that I was unscathed when he stopped and stepped back to a force beyond myself.

We were now a good thirty feet from Jess Hook, who yelled, "Damn it, Cutter! You're killing yourself!"

Cutter did not look well. He was pasty, his face sprinkled with beads of sweat. He swayed slightly as he stood there glaring at me. His lips were drawn back from his teeth so that he seemed more akin to a rabid beast than a rational human being.

What makes people do what he was doing? Why, in the face of all reason, do we ignore what is best for us and do that which will only heap hardship on our heads? Is it pride that makes us think we are immune to the folly of our actions? Or is it that we think we are invincible when we are not? Whatever the cause, I was grateful Cutter was no different from any other mortal; he was too stubborn for his own good.

"Did you hear me?" Jess Hook shouted.

"Quit pestering me!"

"Fine. You're on your own."

Hefting his knife, Cutter crouched. "It's you or me. I won't stop until one of us is done for."

"You should listen to him and let him bandage you." I was stalling.

Cutter cocked his head. "I hate you."

Why he said that, at that moment, was a mystery to me. But it was not all he had to say.

"I hate you more than I have ever hated anyone or anything. You are all that is wrong with this world. You are why I am as I am."

That made no sense whatsoever. I figured the loss of blood had brought on delirium. "We are each of us accountable for our own actions," I responded.

"There you go again, using big words. I hate that, too."

Now I ask you, where was the logic in that? Why hate a person's vocabulary? "What you need is a cup of tea. My grandmother always claimed that calms the nerves."

For some reason that drove Cutter berserk. Roaring like a mad bear, he charged me, his knife weaving a tapestry of death.

I did the only thing I could.

I turned and ran.

A string of swear words blistered my ears as I weaved through the aspens with all the speed I could muster. I risked a look over my shoulder to see if Cutter was after me.

He was.

I had never seen anyone so furious. His face was so red, it was virtually purple. Rage contorted his features. His eyes were filled with red lines, and his nostrils were distended. His chest rose and fell in great gasps.

I am not fleet of foot. Under ordinary circumstances, Cutter would have caught me with no difficulty. But he was severely wounded, and his wound slowed him. I, on the other hand, was spurred by my fear. I ran for all I was worth. Reaching deep down inside of me, I called on reserves of stamina I did not know I had.

"Come back!" Jess Hook bellowed. "You are in no shape for a foot race, you damned fool!"

My adversary paid no heed. He wanted me dead, and he would stop at nothing until he achieved that end.

As if to confirm it, Cutter screeched, "I am going to kill you! Kill you, kill you, kill you!"

Jess Hook did not come after us. Maybe he thought Cutter would be mad if he did, although how Cutter could get any madder was beyond me. I ran and ran, Cutter never more than a few steps behind me. One slip of my foot and he would be on me, stabbing and slicing.

I kept glancing back to be sure he was not gaining. Along about the tenth or eleventh time, I rounded an aspen, and there, directly in front of me, was another. I tried to veer to the right but the tree was too close. I slammed into it and the impact knocked me off my feet.

The next thing I knew, I was flat on my back, dazed and in agony, and Cutter was standing over me, sucking air, half his shirt bright scarlet, his knife poised to finish me off. He grinned in triumph. "I have never wanted to kill anyone so much in my entire life."

I had dropped my knife when I hit the tree. Unarmed and unable to rise, I was as good as done for.

Cutter tensed for the fatal thrust. Suddenly blood trickled from a corner of his mouth, and then from the other corner. A strange look came over him. "No!" he exclaimed, and staggered back a step. "Not like this!" He steadied himself and again raised the knife, only to have a river of red gush over his lower lip.

I was stupefied. Belatedly, it occurred to me that this was a result of my stabbing him. He should have listened to Jess Hook.

I pushed against the ground and sat up. My hand came down on a familiar object, and a second later I held the knife Blue Water Woman had given me. But I did not use it. There was no need.

Cutter's arms had drooped and his chin had dipped to his chest. He groaned, then attempted to speak. But all that came out was a frothy gurgle. His legs buckled and he slowly sank to his knees.

I just as slowly stood. "Do you see what comes of being evil?"

Cutter opened and closed his mouth a few times but all that came out was more blood. A fit of coughing doubled him over. When it ended, he spat and looked up at me. "I can't tell you how much I hate you."

"Do you want those to be your last words?" I asked.

They were. Life fled from Cutter's eyes. Like pudding poured into a bowl, he oozed to the earth, quivered and was still.

I mopped my forehead with my sleeve. My relief,

though, was short-lived. I abruptly remembered Blue Water Woman was at Jess Hook's mercy.

She needed me.

My legs were leaden, but I willed them to move. Each second was an eternity of anxiety. When, at last, I came in sight of Jess Hook's horse, my worry knew no bounds; he was not on it. I sped past more aspens and saw him, on his knees beside Blue Water Woman. She had not revived, and he was slapping her to bring her around.

"Wake up, squaw! I want you to feel it when I do you!"

When it comes to stealth I am a blind cow. But by stepping on the balls of my feet and watching for twigs, I crept within fifteen feet of him without him being aware. He slapped Blue Water Woman twice more, and suddenly she was staring up at him as calmly as you please.

"You have hit me enough."

Jess Hook laughed. "Hell, I am just getting started. For what you did to Jordy you will die a tiny piece at a time."

I slunk forward, hoping I could get close enough to use the knife. But *would* I? The decision was taken from my hands when Jess Hook stood, stepped back from Blue Water Woman, and leveled his rifle at her knee.

"We will start with your legs and work up. Feel free to scream all you want. No one will hear."

I cleared my throat. "I would rather you didn't do that."

Jess spun, his legs spread wide, ready to shoot. Astonishment rendered him mute but only for a few seconds. "You!" he blurted. "Where is Cutter?"

"Dead," I said.

"Not in a million years, mister. Where is he really?"

"Wherever scum like him go to when they give up the ghost." I was trying to provoke him, and I succeeded. He took a step toward me, his finger curling around the trigger.

"If you are not blowing smoke, then I get to make worm food of both of you." Jess tucked his rifle to his shoulder. "You I'll do quick. Smack between the eyes."

Once again I stared death in the face.

Then it happened.

I saw the whole thing.

Blue Water Woman's arm appeared between Jess Hook's legs. Her hand rose to his belt and wrapped around a pistol. He felt her yank it free, and gave a start. Before he could think to grab it, she pressed the muzzle to his groin, the barrel angled up, and fired.

Stars sparkled in the firmament later that night. In the distance a wolf howled. The night was pleasantly cool this high up.

I took a sip of steaming hot coffee. "You are leaving it up to me? Whether we go back down or stay so I can paint and sketch?"

"Whichever you like," Blue Water Woman said. "After what we have been through, I imagine you can use some rest."

"It shows how little you know me," I teased. "Bring on the paint and the canvas."

"You are strange, Robert Parker," Blue Water Woman said.

"Strange as in special?"

"No. Strange as in male. All men are. But we women put up with you."

Her smile made me warm all over.

Postscript

According to his journal, Robert Parker spent three more weeks in King Valley. He named the yellow-crowned kinglet in honor of his hosts.

Nate King took him back to Bent's Fort. There, Parker solved the mystery of the horse covered with blood.

Augustus Trevor had been concerned for the naturalist's welfare, and followed him, intending to keep an eye on him without Parker being aware. What Trevor did not know was that the Hook brothers and Cutter were also shadowing Parker and Zach. To keep Trevor from interfering, one of them shot him in the back. They saw him fall, but when they reached the spot, they could not find his body. From the amount of blood they assumed he would die, and they rode on. But frontiersmen were a hardy breed, and Augustus Trevor was one of the hardiest. Emaciated almost to the point of starvation, he made it to Bent's Fort. The rest of Parker's party immediately set out after him. Since no one, not even St. Vrain, knew how to find King Valley, they had no recourse but to return to the trading post and await his return.

By the time Parker showed up, Trevor had recovered

sufficiently to lead them on a nine week "species tour of the Rockies," as Parker referred to it. His observations, sketches and paintings were lauded in the press and in academic circles. All told, he documented over a thousand new varieties of plant and animal life.

Parker went on to became a professor at the University of Pennsylvania. He eventually headed their Ornithology Department. He was a prominent member of the American Philosophical Society and a fellow of the Linnaean Society, where he rose to the position of vice president.

Robert Parker never married. He led a quiet, scholarly life. For thirty years he lived in a small house near the university. His most prized possession, according to friends and acquaintances, was a painting he hung in his bedroom.

It was not a painting of the birds he loved so much or any of the animals or plants he discovered. It was a painting of a woman, and all who saw it praised it as the best painting he ever did. He was offered large sums of money for it, but he refused to sell. No one ever learned the woman's name. All Parker would tell them was that she was a Flathead.

Enjoy the Wilderness series by
David Thompson
from the very beginning!

Louis L'Amour
Grub Line Rider

Louis L'Amour is one of the most popular and honored authors of the past hundred years. Millions of readers have thrilled to his tales of courage and adventure, tales that have transported them to the Old West and brought to life that exciting era of American history. Here, collected together in paperback for the first time, are seven of L'Amour's finest stories, all carefully restored to their original magazine publication versions.

Whether he's writing about a cattle town in Montana ("Black Rock Coffin Makers"), a posse pursuit across the desert ("Desert Death Song"), a young gunfighter ("Ride, You Tonto Riders"), or a violent battle to defend a homestead ("Grub Line Rider"), L'Amour's powerful presentation of the American West is always vibrant and compelling. This volume represents a golden opportunity to experience these stories as Louis L'Amour originally intended them to be read.

ISBN 13: 978-0-8439-6065-5

MAX BRAND®

Luck

Pierre Ryder is not your average Jesuit missionary. He's able to ride the meanest horse, run for miles without tiring, and put a bullet in just about any target. But now he's on a mission of vengeance to find the man who killed his father. The journey will test his endurance to its utmost—and so will the extraordinary woman he meets along the way. Jacqueline "Jack" Boone has all the curves of a lady but can shoot better than most men. In the epic tradition of *Riders of the Purple Sage*, their story is one for the ages.

ISBN 13: 978-0-8439-5875-1